TROUBLE
AT
LINTON ABBEY

Agnes Blackwood

with Original Illustrations by Curtus

Jacket Illustration by Sardax

AKS
BOOKS
LIMITED

Published 2000 by
AKS BOOKS Ltd.
PO Box 39, Bexhill-on-Sea, East Sussex TN40 1WR

Cover Illustration by Sardax.

Also published by AKS Books:

A HISTORY OF THE ROD
THE ART OF DISCIPLINE
IN FRONT OF THE GIRLS
TALES OF THE UNBREECHED
THE QUEEN OF THE GROVE
OUCH!!
THE SONG OF THE CANE
ACROSS MY LADY'S KNEE
THE LOST BREECHES
TAMING THE HOUSEHOLD BEAST
CHÂTEAU SOUMISSION
and
THE GOVERNESS COMPENDIUM

A catalogue record for this book is available from the British Library.

ISBN 1 899861 21 1

Printed and bound in Great Britain by
Antony Rowe Ltd, Chippenham, Wiltshire

CONTENTS

With this he drew back his palm and slammed it—CRACK!—with the force of an express-train, flat across Howard's bare backside. [P. 3.]

1. The New Arrivals

A S THE big black car made its way through the narrow and winding leafy lanes that led to the tall iron gates of Linton Abbey School, the blonde-haired girl in the back seat checked her reflection in her pocket-mirror one last time, and one last time she saw her new self there: not a West Virginia farm-girl in patched dungarees any more, but an English schoolgirl, a genuine English schoolgirl, looking right back at her.

Fourteen-year-old Laura Wall made a rather smart English schoolgirl, as a matter of fact, and a very pretty one, too: tall and slender and clear-skinned in her starched-and-ironed navy-and-white gingham Summer dress and her whiter-than-white ankle-socks, her black T-bar shoes polished to a mirror shine. Her yellow hair shone sleek and glossy in its two long bunches, tied in pretty bows with new two blue ribbons, and it smelt of shampoo and brushing. She grinned and wrinkled her upturned nose: the English girl in the mirror grinned back and wrinkled her nose, too.

"I say!" she said, looking at her reflection and speaking in her best attempt at an English accent. "Jolly good! Pip, pip, old chap!" and then she remembered where she was, and remembered Howard, the rich New York boy sitting sullenly by her side in his English blazer and his flannel shorts. Laura blushed a little, and coughed as if clearing her throat.

Howard—Master Howard J Franklin III, to give him his full name—gave her a scornful look. "Jeez!" he said, shaking his head slowly; and then he turned his attention back to chewing his gum and watching the scene unfolding outside his window, looking as if there were an unpleasant smell under his nose.

"I hate England," he said, as the car slowed right down to pass a group of girls on ponies. He pronounced the word 'Eng-land', as you might say Disney-land, or Mary-land. "It's a dumb place," he added.

Howard and England had not got off to a particularly good start together, it must be said. The English, he decided, needed to learn a thing or two about man-ners. Had he not won—or at least got his rich father to arrange for him to win—

a prestigious international scholarship? And was he not entitled to a bit of respect? He elbowed Laura sharply in the ribs: she was taking up too much room on the seat, fussing with her cheap little pocket-mirror, and he wanted to spread out more.

And as for the English… why, he'd even had to carry his own brand-new leather suitcases, himself, a whole twenty yards from the station to the car sent to collect him, while—to really rub salt into the wounds—both the station porter and the Linton Abbey driver had fallen over themselves to carry Laura's battered old bag for her.

And the pony-girls outside the car window looked so very smug and so very English in their stretch fawn jodhpurs and their tweed hacking-jackets, and their crisp white shirts and smart ties, and their dark blue velvet-covered riding-hats; that just the sight of them made Howard feel even crosser than he already was.

Laura, on the other hand, felt even happier, though she tried as best she could not to let Howard see. She loved horses and ponies more than almost anything in the world; and the chestnut ridden by the lead girl reminded her so much of Chuck, her own pony back on the farm, that she almost wanted to get out right there and then, and jump up onto his back.

The girls peered in as the car edged slowly by them, and smiled and waved their crops. Laura smiled and waved back: Howard didn't. In fact, he turned right round and stuck his tongue out at them, as far as it would go.

The smiles froze on the girls' faces. And as the car overtook them and pulled slowly away, Howard hooked his fingers into the corners of his mouth, rolled his eyes and pulled the most grotesque grimace he could think of.

The girls, trotting a few yards behind the car now, began to look rather cross. This gratified Howard no end; and he noted with some pleasure that the foremost rider, a quite strikingly pretty, haughty-looking young miss with dark hair in a bob, was looking positively furious, and that she seemed to be mouthing some words at him which he couldn't hear; but which he was sure were not at all complimentary; so he took his fingers out of his mouth and did some rude hand-gestures, just for her.

For the very first time since he arrived in England, Howard found that he was actually beginning to enjoy himself: so much so, in fact, that he didn't notice the car coming ever-so-slowly to a gentle halt. Nor did he even notice the grey-uniformed driver getting out of the car; or Laura's horrified embarrassment or anything else at all, until he suddenly found himself being seized by the arm and pulled bodily from the vehicle.

"Hey!" he cried, indignantly.

"I seen you, young feller-me-lad." said the driver.

"Do you realise who I am?" said Howard. This never failed to work back home. For answer, the driver began to frog-march Howard towards the front of the car. The boy was outraged.

"Do you realise how rich my father is?" he protested. "Do you realise I'm here on one of the most prestigious scholarships in your Goddamned country? Do you realise… "

But his protests had no effect. Nor did his struggles. Nor, even, did his attempts to bite the man's hand and kick his shins.

"What I realise," said the driver, grimly, as he dragged the boy along, "is what you is doin' out the window of my car. That is what I realise."

"Oh is it?" said Howard, sarcastically. "And say, what kind of a dumb accent is that, anyhow? Don't they teach you how to talk in this country?"

And with that, Howard found himself seized by the scruff of the neck and flung face-down over the bonnet of the car.

"Hey!" he shouted. "Hey, put me down! You hear me?"

By now, the pony-girls had reached the car. They wheeled their ponies around and reined then up in a semi-circle around the front of the car just as the driver seized hold of the elastic waistband of Howard's shorts.

"HEY, QUIT THAT RIGHT NOW!" yelled Howard, kicking and struggling for all he was worth; but he was pinned down tight, and, with a single tug, both his shorts and his underpants were down around his ankles.

"And now," said the driver, tapping the peak of his cap, first at the pony-girls and then at Laura in the car. "If you young ladies will be excusing me, I'll just see to the young gentleman."

With this he drew back his palm and slammed it—CRACK!—with the force of an express-train, flat across Howard's bare backside.

From where she sat, looking more or less directly at his face, Laura caught the brief instant in which the boy's eyes bulged in pain and shock and horror and rage and disbelief, as if they were going to pop out of his head; before he let out such a shrieking high-pitched howl that she half-feared that the car windows might shatter. She could only guess at the damage done at the other end; the pony-girls, however, had an altogether closer view of that, and watched the rapidly darkening, swollen scarlet handprint appearing across the boy's seat. A satisfied little smile flickered across the lips of the dark-haired girl, who was closest of all.

The driver raised his hand and delivered another—CRACK!—which, if anything, was even harder than the first, and which brought forth from Howard an anguished yowl several octaves higher. Then came a third—CRACK!—and a fourth—CRACK!—at which the boy's tears really began to flow in earnest and his fists to drum against the bonnet, and his feet, dangling uselessly above the ground, to twist and kick and cross and uncross. Then came a fifth—CRACK!—and, despite Howard's tears and cries and pleas, a sixth, hardest of all—CRAAACK!— and then he was dumped unceremoniously in the dirt, sobbing fit to burst and clutching his very bruised, very bare backside.

"Now get up and dress yerself." said the man.

Which he did, but not before—in his haste, and in his rage and humiliation, and flustered by the steady gaze of the pony-girls—he tangled himself up in his under-pants, and tripped over, and cursed bitterly to himself, and somehow became parted from one of his shoes, which he picked up and flung to the ground in temper, and then had to pick up again and attempt to jam onto his foot without undoing the laces and doing them up again (he was far too cross for that); and all the while the semi-circle of ponies stood silently around him, watching, until— when he finally managed to collect himself enough to wrench the car door open and fling himself inside, slamming it behind him, they turned their ponies around as one, and dug in their heels and flicked sharp and smart with their crops, and set off at a rising trot, presenting Howard with an insufferably smug vision of departing English girlhood, all pony-tails and jodhpurs, clippety-clopping off—in the direction, as it happened, of Linton Abbey School.

AND SO to the school itself; or, at least, for the moment, around a sharp bend in the road to the gates of it. The school was some way away yet, despite the announcement of its name in three-inch-high capitals on the polished brass name-plate set into the nearest of the two tall stone pillars flanking the high, spike-topped railings. Co-Educational, said the enamelled copperplate engraving. For Girls and Boys Aged 11—18. Headmistress: Mrs… . But the driver was back in the cab now, having unlocked the lock and swung back the heavy ironwork; and the car was off again. Beyond the gates a broad gravel drive curving across a close-cropped lawn past a low, white gatehouse and then disappearing into a dark forest of gnarled, ancient oak-trees. But of the school, still—of the place that was to be Laura's and Howard's home for the next twelve months—nothing could be seen at all, not even a glimpse. And the wood seemed to go on and on for ever and ever.

When they emerged, at last, from the other side, then they saw it; and when they saw it, the sight of it quite took Laura's breath away.

Up ahead, at the far end of a long avenue of ornamental yew trees, and set in a wide expanse of formal lawns dotted with bowers and arbours and ornamental lakes, stood the school itself, tall and beautiful and grand and classical with its red sandstone pillars and pediments.

To Laura, for whom school back home had been a one-room clapboard cabin where she had been bullied by farm boys in dungarees, and whose learning had largely been instilled in her at the fireside by her self-educated God-fearing grandmother, it was like something from another world.

All around the house, the grounds and gardens were filled with all of the activities of a busy school: groundsmen and gardeners dug and pruned and trimmed; groups of girls and boys sketched and collected leaves and caterpillars for projects; and then there were the sports. There were sports everywhere. Some of them were familiar to Laura: others less so. There was a game that looked to her very much like baseball or softball, being played by two teams of girls in little blue pleated kilts, but using a bat somewhat smaller than those she was used to. There were other girls, dressed similarly but wearing navy cotton tabards over their aertex blouses, with things like GA and GD stitched on them in big white letters, playing a game that looked a little like basketball, except that the girls threw the ball rather than bouncing it. There were boys playing a game that looked very much like football as she knew it, with the familiar oval ball, although they weren't wearing the usual helmets or shoulder-pads.

Everyone looked so nice, and so smart, and so happy and busy. Laura felt that she was going to be very, very happy here.

As for Howard, red-faced and tear-streaked, clenching and unclenching his fists in the seat by Laura's side: well, that is another story altogether.

And meanwhile, way up ahead, a small group of ponies trotted around the main school buildings and off towards the stable-block that lay beyond.

2. The Head Girl

W/HEN THE car pulled up in the courtyard beneath the window of her study, Julia Carstairs, the Head Girl, was really rather busy.

She was right in the very middle of a very important conversation, at the time; and not only that, but she was right in the middle of a word, too, and right in the middle of a particularly important sentence; but the moment—the very moment—that she heard the chugging of the engine, and the rumble of the tyres on the cobblestones, she stopped what she was doing, just like that, right there and then.

"Oh Gosh!" she exclaimed, sweeping back a long, loose strand of fair hair from her forehead and tucking it back into her elastic pony-tail band, and "Oh Golly!" she said.

She dashed across to the big bay window and peered down.

"Oh Crikey!" she said, "I'd quite forgotten."

Julia turned back to her companion, a junior boy of about twelve or thirteen.

"No time!" she said. "No time at all, now. I'll have to dash, I'm afraid!"

The boy said nothing, but looked at Julia with a puzzled expression on his face. This was something of an achievement: he had his back to her at the time, and—not a particularly tall boy anyway—he was right up on his tiptoes bending over the back of her high-backed dressing-table chair. It involved rather a lot of twisting and craning of the neck, but he managed it, nevertheless.

Julia put down the rubber-soled tennis-shoe she had been holding, placing it on the table a few inches from the boy's face.

"You can stay there, Edwards," she said. "I'll be back later."

And with this she snatched her blazer and her straw hat from the rack by the door, and turned on her heel and rushed from the room, leaving the heavy mahogany door open wide behind her and, on her way out, almost crashing headlong into the large group of giggling fourth-form girls who happened to be passing in the corridor at the time, on their way out to afternoon break.

The courtyard was already milling with girls and boys by the time the car pulled up; and there had been a great deal of talk about the new pupils ever since the Head announced their arrival in Assembly; and consequently there was a great press around the vehicle to be the first to catch a glimpse of them. The driver was first out, and he cleared a space to open the passenger door for Laura, offering her his hand to help her out. She was immediately surrounded by pupils offering her their hands to shake, and telling her their names (of which their were far too many for poor Laura even to attempt to remember), and asking her whether she had enjoyed her journey, and whether she liked what she saw of the school so far, and how it compared with what she had been used to back home.

This went on for some time, during which Laura's hand was very nearly shaken from her wrist. Howard, meanwhile, having hastily smeared his face on his shirt-sleeves in an attempt to wipe away as much of the evidence of his tears as he was able to, remained sitting in his place trying to look as nonchalant and as unconcerned as he could, which was not very much at all, what with his stinging bottom and his wounded pride, and what with the huge waves of rage and fury welling up inside him.

And to make matters worse, no-one had come around to open his door for him, or to unload his bags from the boot; and, with all the fuss over Laura, he appeared to have been overlooked altogether. "Well," he thought, "if that's how they want to be, then I'll just stay right on here. And see if I care!"

After a while, a woman appeared at the door of the school. She was an elderly, rather thin woman in a tweed suit, with grey hair in a tight bun at the back of her neck, and horn-rimmed half-moon spectacles on a chain around her neck. Seeing the commotion in the courtyard, she waded her way through the crowd, tweaking an ear here and a tuft of short hair there to move small boys from her path, until at last she reached Laura.

"Aha!" she said, putting her spectacles on and peering at the new girl through them. "And what have we here?"

"Um, I'm Laura, Ma'am, Laura Wall." she replied.

Not having met an English schoolmistress before, Laura did not know quite how to greet one. In the end she settled for a sort of gentle shake of the hand and a little curtsey-like bob, which seemed to her a very British kind of thing to do.

"I'm pleased to meet you, Ma'am," she said.

"Good heavens!" exclaimed Miss Clark. "What extraordinarily polite manners you have, young lady. And your accent... I take it that you are not from this side of the herring-pond, as they say?"

"No, Ma'am," said Laura, raising her voice to be heard amongst the din of the playground. "I'm from West Virginia, Ma'am. That's in the USA."

"Well, Miss Laura Wall from West Virginia, in the USA, I am Miss Clark, from Linton Abbey School, which is in the County of Devon, England. I am the Classics mistress, and I am most pleased to make your acquaintance. And how, exactly, may we be of assistance to you, may I ask?"

"I'm sorry?" said Laura.

Just then, a girl's voice called from the other side of the car.

"I say," she called. "Sorry I'm late!"

Laura turned around and saw a smiling, grown-up girl of about seventeen waving at her as she made her way through the crowd, her long fair hair tied back in a pony-tail.

"I'm Julia," she said, when she reached Laura at last, and she thrust out her hand. "I'm the Head Girl. You must be the new girl. Jolly pleased to meet you."

Laura started to do her little curtsey, but Julia just laughed and shook her hand heartily.

"No need to be quite so formal," she said. "You'll find we're a friendly bunch here."

Miss Clark looked on, puzzled.

"Do you know this young lady, Julia?" she said.

"Yes, Miss Clark," she said, speaking slowly and deliberately, and a touch louder than one might deem strictly necessary, even in a crowded playground. "This is the new EXCHANGE SCHOLARSHIP girl. From AMERICA. DO YOU REMEMBER? The Head reminded us all about her in Assembly this morning."

Julia moved a little closer to Laura.

"You'll have to forgive Miss Clark," she said, in a low voice. "She's utterly brilliant in her field, you know; but sometimes she's not quite with us."

"What was that?" said Miss Clark. "America? Scholarship girl? This morning, you say? Good gracious! The Head herself, you say? Well, I never... but wait! Ah yes! Now that I think of it, I do seem to recall something of the kind. Yes, yes, it is all coming back to me now. It even strikes me that I am to be her form-mistress: is that not so?"

"I believe so, Miss Clark."

"And so this is she?" Julia nodded vigorously.

"Then why didn't you say so, for Heaven's sake."

"I do believe I just did, Miss Clark."

"Well, it was obviously not clearly enough, young woman. You really must learn to enunciate clearly, and not mumble."

She turned to Laura and peered at her through her spectacles. "So, young lady," she said. "Now that I have placed you, I also seem to recall that you were to be not singular but plural, if you will forgive the grammatical allusion."

"Excuse me, ma'am?"

"She means," said Julia. "That there were meant to be two of you."

"Oh yes, there are two of us."

"Exactly!" said Miss Clark. "And so where, pray, is the other?"

And then she caught sight of Howard in the car.

"Good Heavens!" she exclaimed. "A boy!"

3. Show and Tell

T TOOK some coaxing to get Howard to come out of the car, during which time Miss Clark wandered off, muttering something about a pressing need to construe some Latin verbs. And the very minute he did come out he let fly with a litany of grievances and complaints.

"And on top of all of that," he said, at last, sniffing and wiping his tear-stained face with his sleeve. "I had to carry my own bags to the automobile—can you believe that?—and she had hers carried for her, and I have two brand-new king-size valises, and mine are much heavier than her one little bag, and when I asked your driver to take them, he said to me 'Have you got broken arms?' and when I said no, he just laughed at me and said, 'Well, you just pick your bags up, then.' And then... "—he took a deep breath and pointed accusingly at the driver, who was whistling to himself as he unloaded Laura's bag from the boot—"... he physically assaulted me."

"He did what to you?" said Julia.

"He stopped the car and he grabbed me by my arm and he squeezed it so tight he almost broke it, and then he dragged me right out in the road, and... and he assaulted me. Physically."

There were gasps from the pupils, who crowded round to hear.

Julia looked at Laura.

"Is this true?" she said.

Laura nodded. She half-wished that she didn't have to, because the man had been so nice to her, and because Howard hadn't been exactly blameless himself; but the truth was the truth.

"Jenkins!" said Julia, sternly.

The driver looked up and tapped the peak of his cap at her.

"Yes, Miss Julia?"

"A word with you, if you please."

And she took him by the arm and led him through the crowd to a quieter part of the playground; the full-grown man looking oddly stooped and cowed, trotting meekly beside the slight blonde teenager in her school dress and ankle-socks. Howard folded his arms in quiet satisfaction. Now let's see what you have to say for yourself, pal, he thought; and let's see whether you still have a job after this.

It was some time before they came back. Julia led the way, looking grim and determined. The driver followed up behind, now bare-headed and holding his cap in front of him in both hands.

When she reached Howard, Julia paused for a moment and looked into his eyes. "I've spoken to Jenkins, Franklin... " she said.

"It's Howard Franklin," Howard interrupted. "Howard J. Franklin. The Third. Okay?"

Julia continued as if she had not heard him, "And he has told me what he did to you. And what he did was completely contrary to his terms of employment."

Howard looked at the driver, who looked at the ground, obviously avoiding his eye. Howard folded his arms and smirked, waiting for what was going to come next. Laura, meanwhile, could not help feeling sorry for the poor man.

"But Jenkins has also told me, Franklin" Julia continued. "What you did to deserve it. And you did deserve it."

"But... "

"So you thought it would be funny to make obscene and insulting gestures from the window, did you, Franklin? At young ladies?"

"But... "

"Just what did you think you were doing, you rude boy? Let me tell you now, that kind of behaviour won't be tolerated in this school, not ever; not from any boy, scholarship or no scholarship. Now turn around and face the car."

Howard hesitated.

"I said turn around and face the car. Or are you a disobedient boy as well as a rude one? Perhaps we should get Jenkins to deal with you again... "

The driver began to advance towards Howard, who very quickly did as he was told.

In one swift move, Julia pulled Howard's shorts and underpants right down to his ankles, in front of Laura and the assembled crowd; which had grown considerably in number with the return of the school's various netball and rounders teams from the sports practice grounds.

"HEY!" said Howard; making a frantic grab—too late—for his clothing

Julia expertly pinned the boy's arms behind him and stooped down to examine his behind.

"Yes, that does looks a little sore," she said. "But there's no lasting harm done. And let me tell you, Franklin: if it weren't for the fact it's your first day here I would have given you a jolly good spanking myself; and it would be a lot sorer by the time I'd finished with you. Now pull them up, shake hands with Jenkins, and let that be the end of it."

And, in one way, it was—or at least of that particular incident it was. But in another way, it was only the very beginning.

4. A Room with a View

L AURA'S ROOM was beautiful. She had never seen anything quite like it in all her life. It was big and airy and white, with two tall sash windows and long velvet curtains, and a polished parquet floor with Persian rugs. There was an antique wardrobe for her things, and a bentwood hat-stand and umbrella-rack, and clean, crisp white linen on the bed. A panelled door led through into a bathroom, from which a second, identical door led off into another girl's room.

"Well?" said Julia. "What do you think of it?"

"I think it's... aw, gee, I don't know what to say. It's just so gorgeous."

"We thought you'd like it. It's one of our best. And you should like Sarah, too. You'll find you have a lot in common."

"Sarah?"

"Sarah Johnson: she's the girl you'll be sharing your bathroom with. Now, where is that boy?"

'That boy'—Howard—was bumping and stumbling his way slowly up the stair-case, loaded down with his own two very large leather suitcases and Laura's rather more humble one besides. He also had Laura's blazer draped over his shoulder and her straw boater perched rather fetchingly on top of his own school cap. And Julia had had one or two things about her person as well; a purse, a wooden-backed hairbrush, some pens; and rather than carry them herself she had stuffed them all into Howard's pockets.

By the time he finally reached the door of Laura's room he was red-faced and puffing and panting, and beads of sweat were beginning to roll down his forehead.

"Ah, there you are, Franklin!" said Julia; "We were beginning to wonder what had happened to you. Let's hope you're a bit quicker at unpacking Laura's things and putting them away, because otherwise by the time you get up to your bed it'll jolly well be time to get up again!"

She turned to Laura.

"Boys!" she said, rolling her eyes. "Now, do sit down. You must be worn out, you poor thing, after all of your travels."

TO REACH Howard's accommodation they had to climb three flights of stairs. Being a girl—and Head Girl at that—Julia naturally went first, and Howard followed behind, carrying the things.

At each floor, their surroundings became a step less opulent and a step more functional: the stairway narrower, the ceilings lower, the lighting poorer, the carpets more worn.

On the top floor, in what had once been the servants' quarters, they came to a long, low room, lined with two rows of narrow iron bedsteads, each with a small wooden cabinet beside it. The floor was of bare, hard linoleum tiles and the walls were painted in a sort of dull putty-coloured gloss. The room resembled nothing so much as a military hospital from the Crimean war.

"And this," said Julia. "Is where you'll be sleeping."

It took Howard a little while to find his voice.

"Aw, come on, now!" he said, at last. "Aw, come on. You cannot be serious."

"Oh, but I am," she said, brightly. "This is actually one of our better boys' dormitories, you'll be jolly pleased to know. Look, it even has a window. It's not a very big window, but it's a window nevertheless. So, what do you think?"

And Howard told her exactly what he thought, and in no uncertain terms. About the school; about the way he had been treated; about Laura—who, as he put it, was just 'some little hick from some tin shack in some Godforsaken place where they all have green teeth and marry their cousins'; and about his new dorm. Which perhaps wasn't the wisest thing he could have done, under the circumstances.

AND MEANWHILE, in the big white room downstairs, Laura opened one of her tall sash windows to let in the Spring air, and with it the sounds of her new school at work and play—the chirrup of birds on the eaves; the cries and calls from the playgrounds and sports pitches; a distant chanting of—what?—Latin or French verbs, perhaps; the faint tinkling of piano somewhere across the way; and from a room up above a sudden, sharp, repeated cracking sound and—was it?—a high, piping, familiar American voice raised in protest, and growing shriller and shriller as the cracks continued, together with something like the drumming sound of feet on a hard floor. No, perhaps not, she thought. It couldn't be. Not again. She kicked off her black T-bar shoes and lay back on the crisp white linen of her soft bed, settled a pillow beneath her head and lay gazing at her new room in wonder.

JULIA BLEW on the palms of her hands and rubbed them together.

"There!" she said, a little breathlessly. "That should have sorted that little matter out. I take it you won't be complaining that it isn't fair any more, or asking

Howard was loaded down with his own two very large leather suitcases [P. 11]

me again for Laura to be turfed out so that you can have her room instead? No? Jolly good!"

Howard sniffed and tucked the tail of his shirt back into his shorts, then wiped his eyes with the back of his hand.

"Now," she said, brightly. "A few things I need to point out. The usual rules and regulations, mainly. One bedside cabinet per boy, one small trunk allowed under the bed. No more than three items permitted on top of the cabinet. All clothes and permitted personal possessions to be stored neatly, folded where appropriate. All surplus possessions to be handed to Matron, who will arrange for term-time storage. Prep. seven till eight, lights out at eight fifteen—no talking permitted after that time—and wake-up call at six thirty. Any boy caught talking or creating a disturbance after lights-out will be dealt with by Matron. We expect you to keep the dorm tidy and your bed neatly made at all times, and we have regular inspections to make sure it is. There's an hour before breakfast and an hour after supper for your domestic tasks: you'll find out more about those once you've been allocated. There's a list of rules on the notice-board at the end of the dorm."

And so there was: it ran to several pages of dense small type, in which the words 'It Is Forbidden For Boys To … ' and 'Boys May Not… ' seemed to crop up rather a lot.

"Oh," said Julia. "One more thing. I nearly forgot!"

She thrust out her hand towards Howard. Instinctively he backed away from it, but she leaned forward, grabbed Howard's right hand, and then shook it vigorously.

"Welcome to Linton Abbey!" she said.

5. New Friends

IN THE evening, the dormitory was lit by a row of bare light-bulbs that hung from threadbare old-fashioned cotton-covered cables which ran down the centre of the cracked ceiling. They were not powerful light-bulbs, and not all of them worked: some were missing altogether; and yet it was possible—just possible—for Winters, the Dorm Captain, pacing down the aisle between the beds, to read the names from the paper that he held in his hand.

"Rogers, J." he said, pausing by an empty bed. "Not Present," he said, writing the words on the list by Rogers's name.

"He's in detention," called several of the other boys at once. "Miss Clark's office"

Winters made a note on the paper and moved on to the next bed, on which a skinny and rather rat-like boy lay.

"Evans, B," he said. "Present. I see here that you had four whacks of the slipper from Mrs Bailey today."

"Didn't hurt." said Evans.

"Oh yeah?" called a burly, dark-haired boy sitting on a bed a little further down the dorm. "Well, how high you jump when it does hurt, then?"

"Alright, Gudge," said Winters. "No need to rub it in."

Winters made his way down the dorm, pausing at each bed in turn, empty or occupied, noting who was present and who was absent, and reading out notices and requests from teachers for so-and-so to report to their study or classroom at such-and-such a time, or to hand in a piece of overdue homework, or to go to a certain gym or pitch for sports practice.

"Gudgeon, J." said Winters, as he reached the dark-haired boy's bed.

"Yeah?"

"I hear... ," said Winters. "I hear there was some suspicion that you might have been somehow involved in putting worms into Katie Atwell's gym-shoes today."

"They can't prove nothing," said Gudgeon, a broad smirk on his face. "I've got an alibi."

"It wouldn't involve your friend Davies, by any chance, would it, this alibi?"

"Might do." said Gudgeon.

Winters rolled his eyes towards the ceiling.

"Somehow I thought it might." he said.

"Yeah, well, they can't touch me for it."

Which was more than could be said for Blackley, the red-faced, tear-streaked boy lying face-down on the next bed. He'd been seen leaving Miss Clark's classroom shortly before the unfortunate girl had gone in to fetch her things from her desk.

"Golly!" said Winters, looking at his paper. "Blackley—eight extra-hard strokes with the Head of Year's Senior Cane in front of Katie and her friends."

"And I didn't even do it!" wailed Blackley. "I never even went anywhere near her gym-shoes, but no-one would believe me!"

Winters looked long and hard at Gudgeon.

The next bed—the last one before Howard's—was empty.

"William Marmaduke Davies" said Winters. "Where is he?"

No answer.

"Gudgeon, he's your friend—where's he got to?"

Gudgeon took a deep breath.

"Sarah Johnson's room," he said.

There was a moment's silence as the boys contemplated Davies's fate.

"Oh dear." said Winters.

And then he reached the last bed in the row, on which Howard lay.

Just then, there was a creak on the floorboard in the corridor outside.

"*Cave*" hissed Winters.

"Cah-vay?" said Howard. "What the hell's cah-vay?"

But no-one took any notice: the Latin warning sent all of the other boys diving into their bedside cabinets to pull out serious-looking prep books.

"I said… " said Howard, speaking louder.

Winters clamped his hand over his mouth.

"No time to explain," he said, and rammed an upside-down French Grammar primer into Howard's hands.

And at that moment the door burst open and a short, fat and furious-looking boy in flannel shorts strode in.

"It's okay, chaps," said Winters. "It's only Davies."

"Flaming Sarah flipping Johnson!" said Davies, slamming the door behind him and giving the nearest bedstead a good kick. "Just who does she think she is, eh? Eh? You just tell me that. Just who does she think she is, with all her airs and graces, and her flaming 'Come here, boy!' and her flipping 'Stand in the corner, boy!' and her 'Fetch this, do that, carry those'? I'm flipping fed up with her. Right up to here."

"Yeah, right up to there," said Gudgeon, in agreement. "He's fed up, alright?"

It seemed that agreeing with his friend Davies was one of Gudgeon's main functions in life.

Davies gave the next bedstead an even harder kick, and then flung himself down on the itchy blanket covering his own thin mattress, causing the sagging rusty bedsprings to squeal alarmingly.

"I'm fed right up with the whole flaming lot of them!" he said.

And then he caught sight of Howard.

It is difficult to say quite what went on between the two boys in those first few moments. It may have had something to do with the looks of profound indignation and irritation on both boys' faces; or with their spoilt boys' pale, soft skins; or with the air of contemptuousness that hung around both of them. It may have been even deeper and more mysterious: there are those who speak of some strange sixth sense by which like spirits are able to recognise each other; but whatever it was, something happened.

"Hullo," said Davies. "You're the new boy, aren't you."

"Sure am," said Howard. He unzipped one of his suitcases and—in spite of Rule Number 113 (a) on the notice-board above his bed—'Boys are forbidden to possess unsuitable reading material'—pulled out a great fat wad of brand-new glossy Marvel comics and handed the top one to Davies.

"Here," he said. "Check this out."

6. And So To Bed

IN HIS BED that night, Howard J Franklin III dreamed of school. He was standing, in his dream, in the middle of the cobbled playground, wearing—he looked down—his navy-and-white striped school pyjamas. No—he looked again—he was wearing his pyjama jacket, which stopped short just below his waist, and nothing below. And his pyjama pants were in the hands of the pony-tailed Head Girl who stood facing him, in her crisply ironed cotton summer dress.

"You naughty boy!" she said.

He tried to snatch the pants back, but missed and fell flat on his face.

"Stupid boy!" said a girl's voice, giggling.

"Horrid boy!" said another.

"Hateful boy!" said a third.

He looked up: ankle-socks and summer dresses. He turned his head to the right: bunches and freckles and plaits. He was—he turned his head to the left—he was in the middle of a circle of English schoolgirls.

"Revolting boy!"

"Rude boy!"

"Bare boy!"

And, all of a sudden—SLAP!—a girl's open hand, hard across his bottom.

"Hey!" he yelled, springing to his feet, as the girl dashed back into the giggling throng; and—SLAP!—another, from behind.

He spun around

"HEY!"

And SLAP! across the side of his leg, and SLAP! across the other, and giggles, and jostling as the girls grew bolder and moved closer.

"Lazy boy!"—SLAP!

"Silly boy!"—SLAP!

"Oh, cross boy!"—SLAP!

"Furious boy!"—SLAP!

Howard charged at the girls, trying to break out of the circle.

"Naughty, naughty boy!"—SLAP! SLAP! SLAP!

"Rude boy! Bare boy!" [P. 18]

"Bad, bad boy!" —SLAP! SLAP! SLAP! SLAP! SLAP!

In his rage, Howard put his head back and yelled with all his might. "NOOOOOO!"

And—pop!—all of the girls disappeared, just like that: all apart from one, that is. She was a strikingly pretty girl, with a haughty expression and dark hair in a shoulder-length bob; and unlike the others, she wore riding kit: fawn stretch jodhpurs and shiny black boots. In her hand she held a long, whippy riding-crop.

She was silent for a long time as she looked him up and down contemptuously; and then at last she spoke.

"You," she said, slowly and deliberately, relishing each word. "Are a spoilt, lazy, wicked, naughty, horrid, hateful little boy."

"GO AWAY!" Howard yelled. "GO AWAY RIGHT NOW!"

And Howard was awake, in the dark, cold dorm, and aware of his thin, itchy blanket for just long enough to feel it being whipped away by a matronly-looking middle-aged woman—he rubbed his eyes and tried to focus—in a sort of nurse's outfit.

"What is the meaning of all this noise?" she demanded. And before he could answer she had flipped him over onto his face and, with a single, practised move, pinned both of his arms into the small of his back and whisked his pyjama trousers clean away.

"You naughty, naughty boy!" she said, raising her open palm high above the bed. "Tell Matron to go away, will you? Well, I'll teach you... "

7. The Girl of his Dreams

O NE BY ONE, two by two, three by three, the girls of class 3C strolled and chattered and whispered and giggled their way along the oak-panelled corridor to Miss Clark's classroom, passing at their own pace through the elaborately-pedimented doorway to pull out their chairs from under their desks and hang their blazers and satchels over the backs; and lifting up their desk-lids to rummage inside for exercise-books and pencils. Some girls loitered outside in the corridor, caught up in their conversations, while the boys stood silently by, watching and waiting.

That the boys should stand and wait, and that they should do it in silence, was a School Rule. Before the start of any lesson, the rule said, all boys were expected to form a neat and orderly line to the left-hand side of the door. And it was always to the left: never to the right: the rules were most particular about this. There was a even a little mnemonic or *aide-memoire* in the Rule Book, to help the boys remember it. It was this: Boys Are Never Right. At Linton Abbey it was felt to be quite a useful little mnemonic, as those things went, and to have all sorts of applications that went beyond its original queuing-outside-the classroom use. Jenkins the school driver, who also doubled up as Jenkins the school Caretaker and Jenkins the school Porter, Cleaner and General Handyman, amongst other things, even swore by it as a formula for electrical wiring, of all things: "If you is changing a plug", he would say. "Then Blue is always going to the left, and never to the right; and the colour that is closest to red—which as everybody is knowing is the colour of Girls—that is always going to the right. So you see," he would say. "Boys Are Never Right: that's Science, that is," as if plug-wiring were on a level with nuclear physics; and as if the International Plug-Wiring Committee, or whoever it was who decided the rules on these things, had settled on this arrangement on purpose, for this very reason; and nothing anyone could say would ever persuade him otherwise. He was a simple soul, it must be said: utterly loyal and tremendously hard-working, but simple nevertheless.

Besides the useful little mnemonic, there were a number of other ways of ensuring that boys queued up in the right way before lessons. Most of them tended to be variations on one basic theme, which was the Sore Bottom; but they were all of them remarkably efficient.

Once in their queue, boys were to wait quietly, and without fidgeting, until the last girl was comfortably in her seat and the class teacher had arrived and sorted out her things for the lesson. Only then was the signal given for them to enter.

On this day, as it happened, the first full day the two new pupils had spent at Linton Abbey, Laura Wall had joined a small group of girls lingering in the corridor, deep in conversation; and Howard was second in line by the classroom door, between Davies and the hulking great Gudgeon.

"And it's simply wonderful that we're neighbours now!" one of the girls was saying. "We'll have such a lot to talk about."

The girl had her back to the line of boys; and Davies took the opportunity to turn to Howard and Gudgeon and mimic her, rolling his eyes and wobbling his head about as he mouthed her words.

"And I've got all sorts of things to show you." the girl enthused (and Davies mimicked) "Why not drop by after lessons this afternoon?"

"Oh, I'd love to!" said Laura.

"Oh, I'd love to!" mimicked Howard silently, getting into the spirit of things.

From around the corner at the far end of the corridor came the distant clickety-click of adult footsteps approaching.

The girls looked around.

"Sounds like Miss Clark," said the first girl. "We'll talk later," and she turned to the classroom door; and then immediately froze, stock-still, at the sight of Howard.

And if it was a shock for her, then it was all the more so for Howard, confronted, as he was, with the girl of his dreams; or, to be more accurate, the girl of his fevered nightmare.

She was a pretty girl—a very pretty girl—with dark hair in a bob, and dark eyebrows, and big hazel eyes, and a shield-shaped enamel Prefect's badge pinned to the lapel of her blazer; and there was a haughty look about her; the same haughty look, in fact, that she wore when she looked down at him from the back of a chestnut pony in the lane outside the school gates.

The girl regained her composure in an instant, and looked Howard slowly up and down; then she gave him a brief, contemptuous little half-smile.

"Oh!" she said. "It's you."

Howard was about to say something in reply but Davies clamped his hand over the new boy's mouth.

"You're not allowed to speak!" he hissed.

"What was that, Davies?" said the girl, icily. "Did I hear you speak in the corridor? You do know the rules, don't you, boy?"

Davies nodded.

"Well," said the girl. "We'll have to do something about that later, won't we?"

And then she turned to Howard.

"Well, well," she said. "I didn't recognise you with your trousers on. Still sore, is it?"

And with this she flounced into the classroom, followed by Laura and her companions, leaving Howard purple and spitting with rage.

"Just who in heck does she think she is?" he exploded.

"Sssh!" hissed Davies, urgently.

"But... "

"That," whispered Davies. "Is Sarah Flipping Johnson."

8. Breaktime

"JEEZ!" SAID Howard, as the three boys stepped out into the playground. "*Cogito, Cogitum, cogita…* what kind of a dumb-ass lesson was that?"

"Er… it was Latin, actually," said Davies. "You know, one of the subjects you were supposed to have got top marks for when you won your scholarship to come here."

"Oh yeah, right. Latin."

"Laura was a bit clever though, wasn't she?" said Gudgeon.

"Anyone who can spell their own name is clever by your standards, Gudge," said Davies.

"I dunno about that," said Gudgeon, slowly. "But she was, wasn't she? You know, clever and that."

"I think 'know-it-all girly swot' is the expression you're looking for."

"No, I think he means, 'smart-alec geek'" said Howard.

"Or bloomin'… er… bloomin'… teacher's pet," said Gudgeon, racking what little brains he had for something witty to say.

"Well, you're both wrong, actually," said Davies. "What you actually meant, Gudge, was 'smarmy clever-clogs'. So there."

The boys sniggered.

"Anyway," said Davies. "That's enough of precious Miss Smarty-Pants Laura Wall. That's enough of the lot of them. I don't want to think about any of them: it's break-time."

"Yeah, right. Break time." said Howard. "So let's go and break something!"

And all around and about them in the playground, boys shrieked and whooped and wrestled, and chased each other about, and pretended to be cowboys and indians, or rival armies of knights in armour. Behind pillars, out of the view of prefects and teachers, large boys in long grey flannel trousers twisted the arms and the ears of smaller boys in shorts. And while the boys were busy being boys, little groups of girls were equally busy being girls, talking and playing on benches and in shady spots: the younger ones with skipping-ropes and clapping-songs and handstands-up-the-wall games and the older ones huddled together more quietly, sharing secrets and giggles and schoolgirl gossip.

And the midst of one of these small huddles, on a grassy mound beneath a great Cedar of Lebanon, on the boundary between the cobbled playground and the yew-hedged formal garden, sat Laura Wall.

"Oh, I think it's wonderful," she was saying. "It's like everything I dreamed it would be, only it's better. But… "

She looked around at her companions. They were such nice girls: there was pretty, dark-haired Sarah, of course; and next to her the slender, flaxen-haired Katie Atwell, the sporty one of the three, long-limbed and fresh-faced in her Junior Lacrosse Team kit; and beside her the decidedly un-sporty Hilary Carter, short, ginger-haired, blinking and bespectacled but brainy beyond belief.

"… but I can't help feeling just a little bit sorry. For Howard."

"Howard?" said Katie, spinning her lacrosse stick between her fingers.

"She means Franklin." said Hilary. "She was referring to him by his Christian name."

"Yes, Franklin. And all the boys. Having to obey all those rules, you know; and then being punished—you know, physically punished—if they break them. I mean, I know Howard—Franklin—can be awful at times, but, well… "

And at this moment there was a great indian war-whoop and a yell as a junior boy came charging towards the four girls, pursued by two others pretending to fire pistols at him.

At the very last minute the two pursuing cowboys, or cavalry officers, or whatever they were pretending to be, saw where they were headed and screeched to a halt; but their quarry had turned his head to fire imaginary arrows at them; and by the time he turned back it was too late. He ploughed straight into the little pile the girls had made of their satchels and blazers, sending them flying in all directions, and losing his balance in the process. He tried to right himself, staggering a few paces—which happened to take him right over Sarah's straw hat—and then he lost it and went over and over like a bowling-ball, ending up flat on his back, right into the middle of where the girls sat.

"Oops! Sorry!" he said; and he got up and dusted himself down. He looked around for his friends—but by now they had made themselves very scarce indeed—and saw Sarah's flattened hat, looking like a straw pancake on the ground. He picked it up, pushed the brim back out, gave it a quick wipe on his sleeve, looked at the name-tape on the inside, and handed it sheepishly back to its owner.

"There you go." he said, and turned to leave.

"I don't think so." said Sarah, standing up.

The boy gave an audible gulp.

"… I think you should stand up straight when a young lady talks to you," Sarah continued. "… with your hands by your sides."

The boy—reluctantly—did as he was bid.

"Now," said Sarah. "What's your name, boy?"

"It's Edwards."

"Edwards." said Sarah, reaching out and to take his left earlobe between her finger and thumb. The boy flinched and blinked, and shrank away from her hand.

"My, my. We are nervous, aren't we, Edwards?"

He gulped again.

"Anyone would think that something unpleasant was going to happen to you."

And with this she released his ear and instead began to stroke his cheek with the palm of her hand.

This seemed to make him even more worried, and he began to roll his eyes and twitch under her touch.

"So tell me, Edwards, whose class are you in."

"Miss Parminter, Sarah" said the boy, in a voice that had become almost a squeak.

"Well, Edwards," said Sarah, drawing her hand back a few inches. "I think someone needs to do something about your behaviour, don't you, boy?"

"Y-yes Sarah." he squeaked.

"… And I think we need to start right now."

And with this, she drew her open palm right back and then swung it with all her force—CRACK!—across his cheek.

A distinct red handprint sprang up immediately on his face.

"Did that hurt, Edwards?" she said.

"Yes, Sarah."

CRACK!—another hard slap across his face.

"I didn't hear you, Edwards"

"I said Yes, Sarah. It did, Sarah."

CRACK!

She gave the boy a cold little smile.

"Good. It was meant to. And now I want you to go and see to Miss Parminter in the Staff Room right now, and I want you tell her exactly what you've done. Oh, and Evans… "

"Yes, Sarah?"

"You'd better make sure you tell her everything, because I'm going to check. Now off you go."

She turned to Laura.

"So there you are:" she said. "A typical clumsy, loutish boy. And since you ask, they need rules, and they need to be punished for breaking them because that's the only way to stop them behaving like that—or worse—all the time. I've got three brothers, Laura: I've grown up with them behaving like butter wouldn't melt in their mouths when there's the chance of a spanking in the offing; and then, the minute mummy's back's turned and they think they can get away with it, pinching me and punching me, and calling me all sorts of dreadful names, and not letting me play with them, and threatening me with dreadful things if I tell. Trust me Laura: I know boys."

"I suppose you're right," she said, picking up her blazer and dusting it down. "I suppose I couldn't imagine a girl running into us like that. But... "

"Yes... ?"

"Well, what's going to happen to him now, when he goes to see Miss Parminter."

"She'll probably cane him," said Sarah.

"Or send him to someone who will." said Katie.

Laura was shocked. She'd seen caning in an old black and white film of Tom Brown's Schooldays on the family television set at her grandma's house, one Sunday after church. It looked awful.

"Cane him?" she said, aghast. "But won't it hurt?"

"It's supposed to hurt." said Sarah. "That's what caning's for."

"But hasn't he been punished enough already?"

Sarah smiled.

"You haven't got any brothers at all, have you, Laura? Or any boy cousins?"

"No—but how did you know?"

She chuckled.

"Let's just call it a girl's intuition."

AND MEANWHILE, AS Edwards made his way slowly across the playground towards his caning, Davies, Howard and Evans looked on.

"That girl Sarah Flipping Johnson," said Davies. "is just too flipping big for her boots."

"And that Laura too." said Gudgeon.

"If you ask me," said Davies. "They both of them need taking down a peg or two."

A wicked glint flickered in Howard's eye.

"Too darn right they do." he said.

9. Guided Tour

"A ND DOWN HERE," said Julia, opening the door to reveal a long, gloomy, oak-panelled corridor. "is where you can find the Head."

"A head?" said Laura. "You have a head here? Aren't people frightened?"

She had visions of a real English ghost: a disembodied head, tucked under the arm of a transparent lady or gentleman in Elizabethan costume.

"The Principal, I think you'd call her." said Julia.

"Oh." said Laura. "Of course." She blushed.

Howard sniggered, until a sharp look from Julia silenced him.

"But as it happens," Julia continued. "People do tend to be a little frightened of her. Particularly boys."

The corridor was lined with the usual kinds of things that tend to be found lining important corridors in schools like Linton Abbey: things like framed photographs—some of them very old-looking indeed—of stiff-looking rows of past classes and teachers and teams, with the school crest printed in the foreground; and glass display-cabinets holding various silver cups and shields, and ancient-looking inscribed-and-mounted cricket-stumps and tennis-racquets and hockey-balls; and dark polished oak and mahogany Rolls of Honour, with the names of illustrious past pupils and the dates of their scholarships and prizes painted on in neat Roman script; and a framed photograph of a young-looking Queen Elizabeth II in a tiara and a 1950s dress with a blue sash across it; and a big, dark oil-painting of the Foundress in upright formal pose, in academic robes, holding a scroll in one hand and leaning on a lectern with the other; and—as Laura was beginning to notice about most of the corridors at Linton Abbey—as well as being lined with all of these things, the Head's corridor was also lined with boys.

There were about a dozen boys in the corridor, and they formed a line along one panelled wall to the left—naturally—of the Head's imposing mahogany door.

However, unlike the other boys Laura had seen queuing in the school's corridors so far, these boys did not seem to be waiting for a lesson to start. They didn't seem to belong to the same class, either, or even the same year: scab-kneed junior boys in shorts stood alongside long-trousered young men of Julia's age or even older—the sort of young men who would have been old enough to have stubble on their chins, if the Rules hadn't forbidden it.

The boys in the corridor seemed to Laura to have been deliberately arranged in a variety of poses: some faced outwards, some had their noses pressed to the wall; some held exercise-books or sheaves of notepaper, some stood up straight with their hands by their sides, like soldiers, and others held their hands clasped on the tops of their heads. All of them seemed unusually pale-faced, and all of them seemed preoccupied: and when she smiled at the nearest boy to her, a tall, handsome young man of about seventeen, for some reason he looked down at his feet and avoided her eye.

And then, at the front of the queue, by the Head's door, she saw Edwards, the boy who had crashed into her little group at break-time, standing there in his shorts and shirt with his hands on his head, the outline of Sarah's hand still visible on his cheek and, in addition, with the crimson prints of another, slightly bigger hand showing on the sides of his legs. He seemed to have been crying, and looked as if he were trying hard not to cry again. Then the door of the Head's study opened a fraction, and a deep female voice said "NEXT!" and Edwards disappeared inside, closing the door behind him.

10. A Tea Party

S ARAH JOHNSON SAT in the big wing-armchair by the fireplace in the room
next-door to Laura's. She was still in her stretch fawn jodhpurs and her white
cotton shirt and blue-and-white tie from her ride after tea. She sat sideways
across the chair, her back against one horsehair-stuffed arm and her knees over the
other. Her brown tweed hacking-jacket with the green-and-gold prefect's badge
on the lapel lay spread across the foot of her bed; her elastic-sided jodhpur boots
lay by the door where she had taken them off, and her hat and crop lay on the bedside table.

She was reading a book. It was a slim, blue, cloth-bound volume, and she was
reading it with relish. Every now and again, when she reached a particularly enjoy-
able part, she would mouth the words silently to herself, moving her lips slowly, as
if savouring the feel of them in her mouth, and a satisfied little smile would flicker
across her face.

There was a hand-written label pasted on the front cover of the book: it said
"Form 3 Prefects' Punishment Book."

Sarah really was a very pretty girl indeed. It was a fact that everyone agreed on.
Even the most hateful and repulsive of the boys in the dark-haired junior prefect's
class were forced to admit it. And, as it happened, Sarah herself had forced one of
these very boys in to admit it that very afternoon in the corridor, after first giving
him a good slapping and then pinching his ear and twisting it until he squealed,
and making him thank her for the privilege.

There was a knock at the door. Sarah ignored it.

The knock came again, a little louder this time.

"I'm busy!" she shouted, crossly. "You can jolly well stay there until I'm good
and ready for you. Do you hear me?"

"Okay… " came a girl's meek voice from outside. "I'm sorry I disturbed you. I'll
just stand by the door here, okay? Or I can go away and come back some time later
if you like… " The voice had a distinct American accent.

Sarah snapped her book shut and sprang to her feet.

"Hey! Hang on a minute!" she called.

She ran to the door and flung it open.

"Oh, Laura, I'm so sorry," she said. "So very sorry. I do hope you don't think
me rude: I just thought you were someone else, you see. I'd never have shouted
like that if I'd known. Especially after inviting you round. Do come in: please do."

Sarah's room was a mirror-image of Laura's; except that it was all the nicer, if that were at all possible, for having been lived-in and cared-for, and for being filled with a girl's most cherished possessions.

Sarah's most cherished possessions were mostly to do with ponies. Framed photographs of ponies looked down from every wall: there were jumping ponies, ponies doing dressage, loose ponies in fields, ponies with braided manes, ponies being hugged in showgrounds by girls with paper numbers pinned to their chests, ponies standing next to girls holding silver cups; there were girls dressed for pony-riding standing by paddock gates, or sitting on paddock fences pulling amusing faces at the camera, while ponies chewed the grass contentedly in the background; and just about every other combination of girls and ponies and ponies and girls you could possibly imagine. Some of the photographs had silk rosettes attached to the frames, saying things like 'Leominster Foxhounds Point-to-Point. First.' and 'Frinling Agricultural Show. Overall Winner.' And besides the pony photographs and the pony rosettes there were pony things all around the room. There were Julip model ponies, painted to look like the ponies in the photographs, and dressed up in real miniature tack, with little leather saddles and bridles and little miniature horse-blankets over them. There were several of the silver cups from the pictures, in real life, on a sideboard. There were snaffles and bits, and a curry-comb, on a chair by the door, and there was a collection of crops and whips and sticks standing in a basket in the corner.

In short, it was a room exactly as pony-mad as Laura's own small room back on her parents' little one-acre tenant farm, only much bigger and grander, and altogether more British.

"You must think me a dreadful monster," said Sarah. "Shouting at you like that, as if you were a… well, as if you were a boy or something. It must have made you want to turn right round and jolly well get straight back on the plane to… to West Wickham or wherever it is."

"West Virginia," said Laura. "It's called West Virginia."

"Well, West Virginia, then. But you don't want to go back there, do you? Not now? Do say you don't!"

The two girls' eyes met; and quite suddenly, and quite without bidding, both of them began first to smile at each other, and then to grin, and then to giggle, and then to laugh and laugh and laugh until they were quite hoarse and breathless.

There was a second knock at the door.

"I'd better go and see this time," said Sarah. "Knowing my luck it could be Miss Clark, or even the Head, and Heaven knows what a scrape I'd get into if I shouted at them like I did at you."

She crossed the room and opened the door.

"Oh, it's you, is it?" said Sarah, crossly, her hands on her hips.

Laura couldn't see who it was that Sarah was talking to, but it was very clear that she wasn't very pleased with whoever it was.

"… And what time do you call this?" she continued.

"Half-past six."—a boy's voice—"… the time you told me to come, actually."

"I beg your pardon?"

"I said, the time you told me to come… "

"Are you being cheeky, boy?"

"I'm just stating the fact… "

"I have been waiting for you for ages." said Sarah. "Now get inside, you little brat!"

There was a little squeal, and then Laura came back into the room, pulling Howard's tubby friend Davies by his ear, which she was twisting with some considerable force. Whether the boy was a brat or not—and Laura had begun to form the impression, by what she had seen of him so far, that he most probably was—she could not help but notice that 'little' wasn't perhaps the most apt description of Davies: without his blazer on, she could see that he filled his white school shirt and his grey flannel shorts almost to the point of bursting.

"And you can apologise to Laura."

"You want me to apologise?" he said. "And may I ask what for?"

"Don't push your luck, boy: just apologise."

He looked as if he were about to speak again, but then appeared to think better of it. This may have had something to do with Sarah seizing her riding-crop from the bedside table and holding a few inches from his face.

"I'm very sorry, Laura." he squeaked.

"Good," said Sarah. "The book's on the table."

There were actually several books on the table: almost all of them had pictures of ponies on their covers. Davies went straight to the only one that hadn't, the cloth-bound Punishment Book that Sarah had been reading to herself earlier. He picked it up and took it to the far corner of the room, where Sarah's basket of crops and sticks was kept. Then he stood next to the basket and shuffled his feet forward so that his nose touched the wall, and then placed the blue book carefully on top of his head and folded his hands behind the back of his neck.

"Now," said Sarah, turning back to Laura. "Where were we?"

Some time later Katie and Hilary dropped by, fresh from their various after-school clubs. Hilary was carrying a white lab-coat over her arm and a stack of thick hardback books, almost as tall as she was, with pictures of things like test-tubes in laboratory clamps on the dustjackets, and titles like 'Principles of Molecular Dispersion'. Katie, on the other hand, had been playing tennis. She had on her little white pleated kilt, and wore her long, fine hair wound tightly into a bun, ballet-dancer style. In her hand she carried her wooden Maxply racket in its press.

Neither girl seemed at all surprised by the sight of Davies in the corner with a book on his head, or even to notice him, particularly; and even though Katie went right up to where he stood to drop her racket into Sarah's stick basket, her eyes didn't so much as flicker up at him. It was, Laura thought with amazement, as if it happened every single day.

THE BOY WAS called out after a while, to fetch chocolate biscuits on a plate for the girls, and to serve hot tea from a china teapot, which Laura found something of a novelty.

"Oh my!" she said, uncertainly, as the steaming amber liquid was poured into her cup; and "Oh my!" again as it was followed by a splash of milk from a china jug, and a white sugar-lump from a little pot.

She held the cup hesitantly by the saucer.

"What's the matter?" said Katie. "Never had tea before?"

"Oh no, sure I've had tea before, but… "

"Yes?"

"Well, but never like this. We have it with ice, and no milk."

"Just give it a try," said Sarah.

She took a little sip.

The others watched.

She took a second sip, slightly bigger this time.

Even Davies, back in his corner, craned his head around, until Sarah shot him a reproving glance.

Suddenly, Laura's face broke into a broad smile.

"I love it!" she said.

And although the brew was still scalding hot, Laura drank her entire cup in a matter of minutes.

"Fancy some more?" said Sarah.

"Yes please!" said Laura.

Sarah snapped her fingers.

"Boy!" she said, sharply. "More tea for the young lady."

Davies made his way over to the tea-pot, which was on the table a few inches from Sarah's hand.

"Quickly, you lazy boy!" said Sarah. "We haven't got all day to wait for you, you know."

PONIES WERE of less interest to Katie than to Sarah and Laura, and of no interest whatsoever to Hilary, so they spoke about other things: about lessons, and mistresses and other girls; and, since Laura was still a little puzzled by the subject, bout the way the boys were treated at Linton Abbey.

"But what about him," she said, pointing to Davies in his corner. "Why is he there in the corner like that?"

"Oh, general stuff, really," said Sarah. "It keeps him out of the way, and when I call him he can serve the tea, and clean up afterwards and things. I'll probably have him polish my shoes for the morning, and lay my uniform out for me."

"But what I mean is, what has he done? To deserve it?"

"Done?" she smiled indulgently at Laura. "He hasn't 'done' anything—or at least not anything he's been caught at, which isn't quite the same thing. If he had done something he'd soon know about it! He's here because I'm a girl, and a prefect, and he's a boy and my... well, I would say 'fag', which is the English expression for it, but I think it means something else where you come from. He's here because that's what he's for. It's his job. He's here to do exactly what I tell him to do."

"Like cleaning the floor," said Katie.

"Oh yes! Do you remember that?"

Katie giggled.

"Last term," said Sarah. "I had him clean the floor. With his toothbrush."

"Oh my!" said Laura.

"Yes, but that's not the funny part. He had a dorm inspection that day, and of course his toothbrush was a dreadful state. He tried to blame me for it; but of course I denied everything. He got in dreadful trouble for it, and I got to watch. He didn't sit down for a week!"

"But isn't that... well, just a little unfair?"

"Unfair?" said Sarah. "Well, you could say that if you didn't know him. But that boy," she said, pointing to Davies. "Is the most devious, sly, wicked brat you could possibly imagine."

"Really?" said Laura, her eyes widening.

"Oh yes. And if he does get spanked every now and then for things that he hasn't done, you really, really wouldn't believe some of the things he does do and gets away with."

"He persuades the other boys to do things for him... " said Katie. "And then he lets them take the blame for it when they're caught."

"And they still go on doing things for him?" said Laura.

"Boys are very stupid," said Sarah.

"In conjunction," said Hilary. "With the indisputable fact that Davies's friend Gudgeon is very big."

Katie unfastened her hair from its bun and shook it loose.

"Do you remember the boy who had that fearful caning for putting those worms into my gym-shoes?" she said.

The girls paused for a moment at the thought of Blackley and his recent beating. Katie paused for a moment longer at the thought of the horrible squashy feeling under her toes.

"Well," she continued. "It happened the very next day after I reported that boy there,"—she pointed at Davies—"... for being rude and disrespectful to me."

"Everyone knows he was behind it." said Sarah.

"But no-one can prove a thing, can they?" came the muffled voice of Davies from the corner. "... and until they can, anyone who thinks otherwise should jolly well keep their opinions to themselves."

In an instant, Sarah was on her feet.

"WHAT did you say, boy?" she said.

She snatched up her crop.

"Oh, you are going to regret this SO MUCH!"

"I think you'll find," said Davies calmly, and without looking round. "That prefects are only permitted to administer corporal punishment where there has been a clear breach of the School Rules. Or at least that was what the Rulebook said the last time I looked at it. And I could be wrong, but I don't actually think that pointing out that you need evidence to blame someone for something is breaking the Rules. But perhaps you know better. You usually do. You are a girl, after all."

Sarah stared at him with a look of pure hatred.

"And I don't think," he added. "That your riding-crop is an approved Instrument of Correction. But what do I know?"

For a long time, Sarah did not move or speak. Then, slowly, she put her crop down on the bed.

"That wasn't a very wise little speech at all, Davies" she said, in an icy voice. "I think you're going to live to regret it."

11. A School Tradition

"HE'S HERE," Sarah had said. "Because I'm a girl, and a prefect." But of course it isn't just prefects who have shoes that need to be polished, or beds that need to be made, or rooms that need to be tidied; and it isn't just prefects who have pencils that need to be sharpened, or uniforms that need to be hung up in wardrobes in the evening and laid out ready to wear in the mornings. And, in a busy, sporty school like Linton Abbey, even the most junior first-year gets mud on her hockey-boots sometimes; and since she could hardly be expected to sit down herself with a stiff brush and a tin of boot-polish, and scrub and polish away until her hands are all dirty and sore like a boy's, what she needs is someone to do it for her.

That is why, at Linton Abbey, every single girl at Linton Abbey—prefect or non-prefect—had a boy of her very own assigned to do chores for her; and, why, twice a day, a time was set aside for the chores to be done. Every boy, from the very littlest, squeakiest-voiced new boy to the biggest, most baritone A-level student, was expected to put in a good hour's work each and every morning, weekdays and weekends, before he was allowed to go down for his breakfast. And after he'd done that, and when he'd done all of his day's schoolwork and when he'd sat through any detentions he'd been given during the course of the day, there was a second hour—at least—waiting for him every evening between his supper and his prep. And if the boy was lazy and slapdash with his work (as boys tend to be); or if the girl was fussy and particular (as one or two girls have been known to be, from time to time), then the jobs would just have to be done all over again, and even again and again, until they were done just right. If this meant that a boy's work ate into his breakfast-time, or over-ran into his prep-time, then it was just too bad; and so much the worse for his breakfast, and so much the worse for his prep; and if, as a result, he wasn't properly prepared for his lessons the next day, then so much the worse for his bottom: but he should have thought about that before.

That year, as it happened, there were exactly the same number of girls as boys at the school, which was thought to be a Very Good Thing. It happened that there were three more boys than girls in the fifth form; but by a lucky chance there were three more girls than boys in the first form; so by assigning the hulking great fifth-formers to the first-formers' rooms it cancelled out the imbalance.

There was also a pretty good mix of characters, too, so that—by and large—the most decent, well-behaved boys tended to be assigned to the most sweet-natured girls, whilst boys like Davies were paired off with girls like Sarah Johnson.

There were the odd mismatches, of course, but these were few and far between. The three 'spare' fifth-form boys, as it happened, were a little less than impressed at being at the beck and call of three giggling, freckle-faced twelve-year-olds; but the girls didn't seem to mind too much—quite the opposite, if anything—and so it was thought to be fair enough. One of these fifth-formers in particular, a lad by the name of Duckworth, had what might be described as the interesting fortune to find himself assigned to Nicola Alexander, who was without doubt the bossiest young madam of her year, by a long, long way.

Young Miss Alexander turned out to have some unusual habits, as far as boys were concerned. One of them was her fondness for tweaking and twisting Duckworth's ear at every opportunity, despite the fact that she had to stand up on her tiptoes on a footstool every time she wanted to do it. But if that were all that Duckworth had to worry about, or even all the endless fetching and carrying he was expected to do, or the elaborate, exaggerated respect he was expected to show her all the time as well—the hand-kissing and the 'Yes, Miss Nicola, No, Miss Nicola'—then even then he might have counted himself fairly lucky. But there was something else about Nicola Alexander. Duckworth soon found that however hard he tried to please her; however neatly he made her bed, and however hard he polished her shoes, she always managed to find fault with what he did, and she always—without fail—reported him for it. The result was that once a week, at least, he would find himself summoned up to some office or other, and stood to attention to be told off, and stripped of his fifth former's grey flannel long trousers and sent back to his young taskmistress [PICTURE] with a smarting backside, clothed in a pair of junior boy's shorts.

And as if that weren't enough, young Miss Nicola was always simply bursting to hear all about what had happened.

"And then what did she say?" she would say. "And did she pull them down? What, right down to your ankles? And you had to bend over what, and hold onto what? Go over to that chair and show me how you had to do it. And then she hit you how many times, with her what? And was it very hard? How hard, exactly, would you say? Really? Gosh! And what sort of noise did it make when it hit your bum, and what sort of noise did you make? And did you ask her to stop? How many times? Did you really beg her? Say it now, exactly like you said it to her. And what did she say then? And did you cry a lot, and did you want to rub it afterwards?" And so on and so forth; and he knew, all the time, just what it would all be leading towards.

What it was leading towards was. "… And can I have a look?"

And there was only one answer to that: one answer, that is, that didn't result in his being reported for disobedience: and that answer wasn't 'no'. And so the deep-voiced five-foot-ten teenager would find himself once more standing up straight with his hands on his head in front of a snub-nosed girl a good four years his junior while she slipped her fingers inside the elastic waistbands of his embarrassing little boy's shorts and his white regulation Y-fronts and eased them both slowly down over his hips and thighs; and then he would have to turn his back to her and hear her gasps and giggles as she traced with her fingers the outline of this prefect's tennis-shoe or that teacher's strap or ruler; or even, on occasion, the raised and swollen double-tramlines of a swishy rattan cane.

"So tell me again," she would say, poking a particularly angry welt so hard that it made him wince. "Tell me again about what that one felt like."

12. An Assignment

I T WAS A bright, fresh Saturday afternoon and everyone at Linton Abbey was frightfully busy. Sarah and Laura were down at the stables, where a pony had been allocated to Laura on permanent loan, for the length of her stay at the school. Katie Atwell was playing tennis. Her friend Hilary was pacing around under the great Cedar of Lebanon tree, her head buried in a book about molecules. Julia, the Head Girl, having been duly cross and strict with one or two of the less respectful young men in her year, was now out on the netball courts; and on the Rugby pitch nearby Winters, Howard's dorm captain, was at team practice. It was the sort of day on which every normal, healthy, sensible young person would want nothing more than to be out in the fresh air, doing something thoroughly worthwhile, and preferably energetic. Which is why Howard, Davies and Gudgeon were well and truly indoors, all perched around the furthest rickety iron bedstead in their deserted and dimly-lit stuffy dorm, in the small pool of weak light coming from one of the room's tiny and inadequate windows.

A great pile of forbidden American comics was heaped up on the bed between them, together with the discarded wrappers of dozens of even-more-forbidden Hershey chocolate bars between them. Howard and Davies were reading, whilst Gudgeon—reading not being his forte—was sitting cracking his beefy knuckles.

At this time of this sort of day, in a place where no right-thinking person in their right mind would want to be, they were quite safe from intrusion and prying eyes. Or so they thought; for, quite suddenly, there came a knock—tappety-tap-tap-tap—at the door.

"Jeez!" cried Howard. He sprang instantly to his feet and began shoving as many comics as he could under the bedclothes with one hand whilst scrabbling frantically for a textbook of some kind with the other.

But the other two seemed not to have heard.

"Cah-vay!" hissed Howard, trying desperately to flatten out the big lump his pile of comics made under the bedspread.

Davies looked up amusedly for a moment, and then turned the page of his comic and continued reading

The knock came again, more insistent this time. Neither Davies nor Gudgeon moved.

"Jee-zus!" hissed Howard, trying to force all of the Hershey wrappers into his pockets. "What's up with you guys?"

No reply.

"It could be a teacher," he said, growing more and more desperate. "It could be a girl. It could even be… it could even be Sarah Johnson!" Even in the dim light, the other boys could see that he had gone quite white. Howard gulped. "We could get caned." he said.

Davies seemed to be considering this; and he rubbed his chin, very slowly, to show that he was.

"I don't think so, Howard." he said, at last. "Do you think we could get caned, Gudge?"

Gudgeon gave a sort of slow hur-hur laugh.

The knock came once more, even louder this time.

Davies heaved a sigh of irritation and put his comic down.

"YES?" he called towards the door. "And what do you want, eh?"

Howard looked as if he were about to have a seizure of some kind.

"Er… I've got a letter to deliver," said a voice outside.

It was a boy's voice. Quite a junior one, by the sound of it.

"See," said Davies. "Still think we could get caned, Howard?"

"But… " said Howard. "how did you know?"

"Simple," said Davies. "It's not exactly brain-surgery, you know. Why, even Gudgeon could tell that it wasn't a teacher or a girl outside, couldn't you Gudge?"

"Yeah," said Gudgeon, looking rather proud of the fact.

"And he's not exactly top of the class, now, is he?"

"But… " said Howard.

"It's very simple. We're boys, right?"

"Right."

"This is a third-form boys' dorm, okay?"

"Okay."

"So you tell me who—apart from a junior boy—is going to be lowly enough to have to stand and knock at our door, and then wait outside in a cold corridor until we tell them to come in?"

"Uh… no-one."

"Exactly."

"Er, excuse me please," came a muffled voice from outside the door. "Please may I come in with the letter?"

"Bring him in, Gudge," said Davies. "And let him know that we don't like impatient juniors, while you're at it."

Gudgeon loped off down the dorm, flung the door wide open and, after a brief altercation, came back pulling young Edwards—the boy who had blundered into Sarah and Laura's chat some days before—by the short hair just above his left ear. He was holding an envelope bearing the school crest on it.

"Who's it for, Edwards?" said Davies.

"It's from the Head, for Franklin," he squeaked.

"It's Mister Franklin to you, Edwards. Isn't that right, Howard?"

"Too darn right it is!"

"Gudgeon, would you... ?"

Gudgeon let go of Edwards' hair and took his arm instead. Pushing up the boy's sleeve, he grasped the skinny bare forearm with both his hands and twisted them hard in opposite directions.

Edwards let out a loud, piercing squeal.

"Ah yes," said Davies. "The Chinese Arm-Burn. One of Gudge's favourites."

"Does he have other favourites?" said Howard.

"Oh, he has loads. Would you like to see some?"

"Sure would!"

Some twenty minutes later the weeping Edwards was propelled out of the dorm by a firm size-ten boot up the backside.

"Jeez!" said Howard. "And people say that Gudge has no imagination."

"How very wrong they are!" said Davies.

Hur-hur-hur, said Gudgeon.

"Now," said Howard. "Let's open the letter... There! It says... It says... Yee-ha! It says they're going to give me a room of my own!"

"Never!"

"Naah."

"Sure does. Look, it's here in black and white. 'This is to inform you'—and look, that's me: see my name, Howard J. Franklin III—'This is to inform you that you have been assigned to Bedroom 12 in the Main Building'. That's downstairs! That's on the first floor! So that's it! It's goodbye dorm! Goodbye scummy mattress and threadbare sheets! Goodbye draught from the door! Goodbye goody-two-shoes dorm captain Winters! Goodbye Matron's Inspections. Darn! Do I feel good, or do I feel good?"

Davies and Gudgeon stared at Howard open-mouthed.

"See!" said Howard, handing Davies the paper. "You take a look. But hey!

We're buddies, aren't we? You and me and Gudgeon. I want you to know that won't stop when I get my room. You can visit me whenever you want. Anytime. You just say the word. But sheesh! am I happy, or what?"

"Howard," said Davies, quietly "I don't think that's quite what the letter means."

AND DOWNSTAIRS, in Room 12, a letter sat unopened on the mahogany writing-desk by the tall French windows. It was addressed to Miss Laura Wall, and it said "This is to inform you that you have been assigned the following boy to assist you with your personal needs: Howard J. Franklin III, Class 3C."

13. Howard Starts Work

A KNOCK at the door.

Laura, all of a flutter, ran to answer it.

It was Howard.

"So... um. Hi." She said, awkwardly.

Howard stared straight at Laura said nothing.

"Yes" said Laura. "Well, it was kinda good of you to come. You know. Thanks."

No answer.

"Well, come in."

He did.

"Thanks." said Laura. "Just make yourself at home. Uh, I don't really need much done today. But maybe you could just kind of... dust the coffee-table, or something, and that'll be all for today. I think I've got a duster somewhere... "

But Howard wasn't playing the game.

He flung himself down in Laura's armchair by the fireplace, put his feet up on the coffee-table he was meant to be dusting, and sat there glowering at her. And Laura, fumbling around for the duster she had put down a few minutes earlier, could feel herself growing redder and redder and more and more flustered.

"Can I fix you a drink?"

No reply.

"Would you like a cookie?"

No reply.

It was then that Laura caught sight of the soft yellow cloth she had been looking for; which, to tell the truth, had been staring her in the face all along but which she had been too flustered to see.

"Ah!" she said. "The duster. I don't suppose you want to... ?"

She half-held it out towards Howard, an apologetic look on her face. To her surprise, Howard got up from his chair, made his way over to where she stood and took the cloth from her. For a moment he held it between his finger and thumb, examining it as if he had never seen or touched one before (which was pretty much the case); and then he let it fall to the ground.

"You suppose right." he said.

And then he crossed to Laura's bookcase and took down a book. Then he went back to the armchair, put his feet back up on the coffee-table and began to read. And that was all the work he did, and that was all he would say. And the next night he did and said even less, and the night after that, and the night after that. And so it went on, day after day and week after week, and Laura faced every evening with mounting embarrassment and dread, with her nerves increasingly frayed and her hands increasingly sore from doing the work herself that Howard so pointedly refused to do. And then something happened.

14. Sarah's Ride

I T WAS late one Wednesday afternoon, five weeks into term, that Sarah Johnson
went out alone on her pony in the woods around Linton Abbey.

In a previous term this might not have been unusual: although Sarah rode with
other girls three or four times a week, there were very few, besides her, who went
every single day, whatever the weather and whatever the time of year; and so she
often used to go out on her own. But that had all changed when Laura started at
the school. Laura was every bit as keen on horses as Sarah, and every bit as dedi-
cated a rider; and—once she had got used to the pommel-less English saddles and
the narrow metal stirrups and all of the other things strange to a girl brought up
in the Western style—she hadalready shown herself to be a remarkably fearless
and accomplished rider.

With other girls, Sarah would have to rein her pony in, or wait at gates until
they caught up, but Laura would be with her all along, pushing her to go faster,
galloping full-pelt down forest paths, though the mud from the horses' hooves
half-blinded them and twigs from overhanging trees whipped at their faces; and
then there were the jumps, the two of them charging side by side towards five-bar
gates, thundering closer and closer until there was no way out, other than over;
and then it would be a dig of the heels, a smack of the crop, and forward in the
saddle holding reins shortened almost to nothing, faces almost touching the
sweating ponies' necks, and up and over, and the hooves would hit the ground the
other side, and on they would gallop.

But on this day, unusually, Laura had said she was busy: too much prep to do,
she said; and also that felt a little too tired to ride: and indeed she did look tired,
and overworked besides, and had looked increasingly so for some days, despite the
fact that she now had Howard to run and fetch for her and to attend to all of her
needs. So Sarah went out alone.

Sarah took the usual bridle-paths, and galloped on the usual straights, and
whipped her pony on when he began to flag; but somehow it wasn't quite the same
without her friend: somehow it just didn't have the same excitement to it. And
then Sarah turned a corner in the path, and saw, some twenty yards up ahead of
her, that a big old beech tree had fallen in the night, so that its trunk barred her
way. She trotted up to take a look. It was a fair-sized tree, about as tall, and about
as thick, laying on its side as the height of a gate. The undergrowth was thick with
brambles on either side of the path, so that there was no way round it. Sarah spun

her pony round and walked back to the corner of the way. She had jumped as high before, but not so deep as well. But to go back the way she had come would have taken her an hour or more. If only Laura were with her!

At the bend she spun her pony once more, and brought him to a halt. She looked long and hard at the fallen tree ahead, weighing up her chances. Then, slowly and deliberately, she tightened her hat-buckle, shortened her reins, took a deep breath and kicked her pony on, first into a trot and then, a few paces later, into a full canter.

Closer and closer she came to the tree, and it loomed larger and larger before her; and then it was right before her, and with a final flick of the crop she was air-borne.

The next thing Sarah knew she was sitting on the ground. Her pony was standing by her side, contentedly chewing at wayside plants. and there was a pain… a dreadful pain in… She jumped up with a yowl, clutching at her bottom. She had been sitting—she did not know for how long—in a mixed patch of brambles and stinging-nettles. And as she clutched at the pain with her hands, she could feel little hard, painful spikes in her jodhpurs. They were… she twisted round as best she could to try to see… they were bramble-thorns. She pulled one out, and let out a sharp little cry of pain and frustration. She pulled out another, and another.

"Ow!" she said, and "Owww!"

"ARE YOU alright there, Miss?" said a voice behind her.

She spun around to see a man in a battered green wax jacket and tweed cap, a shotgun broken over his arm and a Jack Russell terrier at his feet. It was Jenkins from the school Lodge House, in his role as Jenkins the Gamekeeper.

Sarah drew herself up. "Yes thank you, Jenkins.", she said, with as much dignity as she could muster, and resisting as best she could the temptation to rub her bottom and cry. "I am perfectly fine."

"Are you sure, Miss?"

She could feel the tears coming to her eyes.

"Absolutely sure." she said. A sob welled up inside her, but she managed to hold it back enough to turn it into something between a cough and a sniff.

"I've got a cold," she said. "That's all. A cold."

The man stood, looking at her uncertainly, and then took a step towards her.

"That will be all, Jenkins," she said, waving him away; and with this she swung herself back up into the saddle, stifling a cry at the realisation that she still had two or three sharp little thorns still embedded in the tender flesh of her backside, and rode off as quickly as her pony would carry her.

15. *Found Out*

S ARAH LIMPED her way back up the stairs to her room, clasping her bottom with one hand and smearing away her tears with the other, only to be met by an amused-looking Davies at her door.

"Well, well," he said. "We have been in the wars, haven't we?"

Sarah gave him a long look of pure hatred.

"You really think you're funny, don't you, Davies?," she said, at last, in a low menacing voice. "Well you just wait, and we'll see who's laughing."

And with this she barged past him into her room.

"Aren't you going to invite me in?" he called after her.

She spun around on her heel.

"What did you say, boy?" she said.

"Chore time." he said. "I expect you've got all sorts of things you need doing. You always do. Shoes need polishing? Rugs need shaking? Grapes need peeling? Or have you got other things on your mind today? And I couldn't help noticing, on that subject, that you seemed to be rubbing your bottom when you came up the stairs. Surely not... ?"

Sarah stared at Davies for a full five seconds; and then, quite suddenly, and with a speed and force that surprised even her, she swung her open palm with all her weight right across the insolent boy's cheek, where it landed with a resoundingly solid CRACK!, sending him reeling backwards against the wall clutching his face in pain.

"Now face the wall with your hands on your head RIGHT NOW, you horrid, HORRID boy!" she yelled, and she ran back into her room, slamming the door behind her as hard as she could—and sending several pony-club trophies crashing to the floor in the process—before flinging herself face-down onto her bed and bursting into a flood of tears.

IT WAS some time before Sarah could collect herself enough to inspect the damage properly. This she did by standing on her writing-desk chair in front of the big gilt fireplace mirror, pulling her jodhpurs and her navy-blue school knickers down as far as her knees, and then twisting herself around as well as she could to see her bottom.

There were long, deep, sore scratches across it from the brambles, from which little spots of blood still oozed; as well as a swollen, slightly lumpy redness all over from the nettle-rash, which smarted dreadfully; but worst of all were the snapped-off tips of bramble-thorns which remained, like splinters, under her skin, and which she had to pinch out, painfully, one by one using a pair of tweezers, and which made her bite her lip to stop herself gasping or even crying out loud. And when she had finished she threw herself back down on her bed, without even both-ering to pull her jodhpurs, and rubbed and rubbed her wounded backside with both hands, trying to shut out the throbbing, and the embarrassment of Jenkins seeing her in such a state—and worst of all, the horrid, gloating Davies, who prob-ably by now was telling everyone he knew. Oh, how she hated him! And how she hated his smarmy new American friend! Together, the two boys reminded her so much of her two eldest brothers that it was almost unbearable: the same smarmy deviousness, the same thinly-veiled contempt, the same pleasure in her suffering. For years at home she had been teased and taunted, and never allowed to join in her brothers' games. And once—and the throbbing in her bottom brought the memories flooding back—once she had asked and asked her eldest brother Jack to let her play with him down at the end of the garden, and he had just told her to shut up and go away and play with her dolls, but she had persisted; and in the end he had grabbed her roughly by the wrist, sat himself down on an upturned bucket, yanked up her skirt above her waist, and in front of both of her other brothers, and in front of Jethro the gardener's boy, a great hairy lout who looked for all the world like Gudgeon, he had spanked her—a girl—on the seat of her knickers, and they had all laughed at her while she cried, and not one of them had lifted a finger to save her. And people wondered why she hated boys so much, and why she pre-ferred horses and ponies instead.

IN THE END, she decided to run herself a bath. She pulled up her jodhpurs and made her way through from her study and bedroom to the door that led to the bathroom she shared with Laura. In the normal course of things she would have knocked before entering, out of politeness and good manners; but she could hear the unmistakable sound of someone scrubbing the bathroom floor inside, which could mean only one thing: that it was only a boy at work in there; and so she just pushed opened the door and walked right in.

And there, to her horror, she saw Laura, down on her hands and knees, scrub-bing away at the white floor-tiles with scouring-powder and a stiff brush; and, worse still, through the open door to Laura's room, laying there on his back on Laura's white bedspread—with his shoes still on—reading a Spiderman comic and belching as he ate Laura's biscuits and drank Laura's orange-juice from a tall glass, was Howard.

16. The Head's Study

THE HEAD sighed.

"You may sit down, young lady" she said.

Laura did as she was bidden, and sat down in the hard wooden chair by the wall, next to the one in which Sarah was already sitting (rather uncomfortably, if the truth be told).

The Head was a sturdy, stocky-legged, ruddy-faced woman in her late fifties, still looking every inch the hearty, somewhat less-than-academically-distinguished English Schoolgirls' Hockey International she had been forty years before.

"You must learn from this," she said, rummaging in a great tall cupboard at the back of her panelled study and pulling out an old brown leather golf bag.

"Yes, Headmistress," said Laura, in a small voice. "I promise I shall."

"Make sure you do. I have seen far too many silly girls mistake this kind of foolish behaviour for kindness, and it never works. Never."

"Yes, Headmistress."

"I do not know what the custom is where you come from, Miss Wall: for all I know the boys in your country are free to do whatever they please, whenever they like. Perhaps they idle away their days chewing gum and swapping baseball statistics when they should be receiving an education. Perhaps they rouse themselves from their idleness only to pull the pigtails of innocent girls, and to demand more gum. And perhaps the females of your race allow them to do this: I do not know. But what I do know, my girl, is that in this country, and at this school, we expect certain standards. And you should look and learn by the example. Why, even our most junior girls know how to deal with a lazy boy: young Nicola Alexander, for example... "

And at that precise moment, as it happened, young Nicola Alexander was dealing with a lazy boy. Or at least, she was dealing with one if you define "lazy" as allowing one tiny speck of dust to settle on a pair of girls' school shoes he had just spent the past hour on his knees frantically polishing and polishing to a mirror shine, while their owner lounged in an armchair eating grapes and resting her feet on his back. And at that precise moment, after sending the boy down to a prefect to be soundly beaten for his monstrous idleness, Nicola Alexander was making him show the marks to her friends in the corridor outside the junior girls' day room...

"I'll try," said Laura. "I promise I will."

"Hmmmph!" said the Head, unzipping the top of the bag and taking out a thin,

Nicola was making him show the marks to her friends in the corridor. [P. 49]

flexible yellow crook-handled stick which she swished through the air several times and then placed carefully on the green leather top of her big mahogany desk.

"Hmmm." she said, rubbing her chin.

So this, thought Laura, was The Cane that she had heard so much about. She shivered at the thought of the damage that the whippy stick might do.

The Head pulled out another cane and swished that through the air. It was slightly thicker and slightly less flexible, and had a slightly lower pitch to it. She rubbed her chin again, not quite convinced, it seemed, by the qualities of the cane, and then placed that one down by the first one, and drew out another, and then another, testing each in turn and appearing less than happy with all of them.

The final cane in the bag was not like the others. It was longer and thicker than any of them, and darker in colour: almost a walnut brown, where the others had all been of various shades of yellow. It was also considerably stiffer when whipped through the air, and made a sort of low whooshing sound.

And now the Head began to seem interested, at last.

"Aha!" she said, and gave it another swoosh. "A-ha."

She took a pace back and touched the end of the cane to the leather top of her desk; then raised it up a foot or so and brought it smacking down with some force. It hit the desk with a loud CRACK!, causing both Laura and Sarah to flinch; causing the pens in the writing-stand on the far side of the sturdy desk to jump and jingle; and bouncing several of the laid-out canes up into the air and off onto the floor.

"That's the fellow!" she said.

It was at this point that Howard began to look very worried indeed: even more worried, in fact, than he had looked ever since Sarah had dragged him all the way down the stairs and through the school to the Head's office by his ear, with Laura following along behind, and with scores of passing pupils stopping to watch their progress. Even then, he already looked more worried than he had ever done in his entire life. But one of the reasons that Howard looked so very, very worried now was that he was being treated to probably the closest view of all of the cane and its effects, bending, as he was, across one end of the desk with his shorts and under-pants and—for some reason—even his long grey woollen socks, all pulled down around his ankles.

From where the two girls sat, a few feet behind Howard's bare bottom, they could see the goose-pimples raising up all down the boy's legs, and the muscles in his backside twitching repeatedly, as if he had developed a nervous tic. Laura sat up very straight in her Summer dress and blazer, biting her bottom lip and squeezing her hands together nervously in her lap: Sarah, on the other hand, still dressed in her jodhpurs and boots, sat back—despite the smarting in her own backside—with her arms folded across her chest and a strangely satisfied little smile on her lips.

"You may count them, boy," said the Head; and without further ado she touched the tip of the cane to Howard's bottom, smacked it lightly a few times against the bare flesh—tappety tappety tap—and then drew it right back and whipped the boy—swoosh-WHAPP!—with all her strength.

Howard squealed with pain and clutched frantically at his wounded flesh.

"Owwww!" he yelled. "Owowowowow!"

"Hands away, boy" said the Head. "And as I said, you may count them. Aloud, if you please. As the Bard himself once said, ye shall count them all out, and ye shall count them all back in again. Hamlet, I believe."

Laura was sure that the Bard had never said anything of the kind, in Hamlet or anywhere else, but she thought it best not to interrupt.

"One… " whined Howard. "But please, *pleeease*… "

"Hands away, boy. Now!"

He moved his hands slowly and hesitantly away, to reveal a thick, raised, deep purple welt which had had appeared as if from nowhere, crossing both buttocks.

Another stroke—swoosh-WHAPP!—across the soft, quivering white skin, just beneath the mark of the first; another agonised howl; hands clamped tight for the second time across the wounded bottom; another command to count the stroke out loud, and to move the hands away. This time Howard took longer to do as he was told, and he begged and pleaded and pleaded and begged that he had had enough, and that he couldn't take any more, and *pleeease*… .

"You should have thought about that before, shouldn't you, boy? Six strokes is your punishment and six strokes is what you will get."

At this, Howard began to cry.

Swoosh-WHAPP! This third stroke seemed to lift Howard almost off of his feet and over the desktop, so that he ended up half-lying across it. More howls and tears and entreaties.

"Hands away, boy." said the Head. "And count them, or else we'll start all over again."

Swoosh-WHAPP! Four.

Outside in the courtyard the fourth-year girls' netball tournament was in progress. Or rather, it had been in progress until Howard's caning began; but then the swooshing and the howling and the crying and the pleading coming through the Head's open window proved so distracting that the girls found it hard to con-centrate; and passes were missed and goals were funked, and defenders were looking around behind them towards the school when they should have been looking in front of them towards the opposing team; and in the end Miss Parminter, the Games Mistress, ordered them all to put the balls down and to sit patiently on the pitch-side benches (what Laura would have called "bleachers") until it was all over.

Swoosh-WHAPP! Five.

Dozens of pony-tailed girls in little navy kilts and short-sleeved aertexes flinched involuntarily, and exchanged glances and nudges and whispers and silently mouthed 'Ow!'s, before settling back down for the next one, bare elbows resting on bare knees, chins resting on hands.

Swoosh WHAPP!

Owoooooooooo!

Back in the Head's study, Howard was stretched out over the Head's desk, shuddering with great sobs, his bottom by now a corrugated mass of fat, angry welts.

"That concludes your punishment." said the Head.

The sound of a netball bouncing outside.

"Now," said the Head. "For the deterrent."

Three puzzled faces turned to the Head.

She swooshed her cane through the air.

"This," she said. "Is intended both for you and for other boys like you, to warn them of the follies of their actions. And it is important for a deterrent that justice is both done, and that it is seen to be done. I am now going to cane your legs, so that everyone who sees you in your shorts will know what has been done to you."

She swooshed the cane again.

"But I really can't take any more," Howard wailed. "Please I can't. I really, really can't."

"Six strokes." she said. "From the tops of your thighs right down to the backs of your calves."

Sarah raised her hand.

"Yes Sarah?" said the Head.

"Please Headmistress… " she said.

"No, Sarah. It is laudable of you to be concerned for this boy, but he has committed a most serious offence and he deserves to be most severely disciplined for it."

"Oh no, Headmistress," said Sarah, a glitter in her eye. "I am sure that he does. In fact, I think he deserves everything he gets. No, I was just going to offer to hold his hands down for you. So that he won't keep getting them in the way."

17. A Poolside Audience

THE GIRL IN the green Lycra bathing-costume squeezed the poolwater from her eyes, pushed back her wet hair, and pulled herself up on the pool-edge with both arms, kicking and splashing with her feet until she was half out of the water, her weight supported by her straight arms and by her lower tummy on the white tiles.

She blinked, once, twice and then opened her eyes wide at the sight ahead of her.

"Oo-er!" she said, out loud.

Behind her, two more girls in green costumes breast-stroked to the edge, followed by four more, and then another two, and then a final one, dog-paddling sedately behind, her head held as high out of the water as she could manage.

The first girl turned back to her companions.

"Look!" she said; and one by one, two by two, each girl hoisted herself up unto the pool-edge, so that they formed a line: and—from across the pool, where their gym-skirted teacher stood, her chrome whistle hanging on a broad red ribbon around her neck—they resembled nothing so much as a line of identical twins; of identical triplets; of identical quads: ten dripping heads of long hair, all turned the same dark brown by the water; ten green swimsuits clinging to the contours of ten narrow backs; ten neat, pert, pushed-out bottoms; and ten pairs of legs dangling down into the water, paddling slowly to and fro.

THE VICTORIAN Public Baths in the market-town of Tivercombe were not quite in the same league as Linton Abbey's own modern Olympic-sized swimming-pool. They were not nearly so big, or so clean, or so well-maintained. Also, they were crowded. Midweek, it was common for two or more parties from the local State schools to have to share the facilities with each other, and with paying members of the public: old grannies wearing rubber bathing-hats, balding bank-clerks in their lunch-breaks and so forth; but it just so happened that on that Thursday morning, as on every Thursday morning, the girls of Class 3C—Howard and Laura's class—needed the school pool for their swimming lesson, and so the boys of Class 3C were herded into the school bus and driven down to Tivercombe.

This is how, one Thursday morning at the crowded Public Baths, as he stood at the back of a queue of boys waiting to dive in, one by one, to swim timed widths under the gaze of the stopwatch-holding Games Mistress, Miss Parminter, the recently-caned Howard J. Franklin III, in his rather tight, wet, navy swimming-trunks, came to be spotted by a row of ten Lycra-costumed young ladies from the second year of Tivercombe Girls' High.

"Hey!" called the first girl. "Hey zebra-legs"

Howard spun around, and all ten girls splashed back down into the pool.

He turned back to his queue, and would have tried to act as normal and unconcerned as he could, if only he could have done something to do so. He would have put his hands in his pockets, if he could have, and whistled a tune, if he could have; if only he had pockets to put his hands in, and if only whistling were permitted. But he didn't, and it wasn't, and he couldn't even "casually" cover up the welts and bruises of his caning with his hands, since there were so many of them, all the way down the backs of his legs; and so there was nothing else for him to do but to stand there, awkwardly, and looking every inch the shamed and whipped schoolboy that he was.

A few moments later the girls reappeared, hoisting themselves back out onto the edge.

Howard pulled at the legs of his swimming-trunks in a vain attempt to hide at least the lower tips of the marks that crossed his bottom, and got a chorus of giggles for his efforts.

He turned around to glare at his tormentors again, and again they disappeared back into the water. From across the pool a whistle blew, summoning the Tivercombe girls back across.

Howard turned back to his queue again, but despite the whistle from their teacher the row of identical swimming-girls reappeared at the poolside.

"Excuse me," called one. "My friend wants to know why you've got stripes on your legs." Sniggers and giggles followed.

"Are they sore?" said another—or perhaps the same one, since it was so hard to tell them apart.

"Aren't you embarrassed, going out like that?" said another—or perhaps it was the first, or perhaps the second.

Howard strode to the pool-edge, his hands jammed furiously on his hips.

"Hey!" he said, as the girls scattered, pinching their noses and all plunging down under the water. A brown head popped up to take a breath, followed by several more.

"You just keep your noses outa this, okay?" Howard shouted.

From across the water the whistle blew again, shriller and more insistent this time.

"Do you hear me?" he yelled.

The girls disappeared back under the water.

He turned back to join his queue, but it was no longer there. All of the boys of his class were now on the other side of the pool; and in their place he saw Miss Parminter, striding purposefully towards him.

"Franklin!" she called, sharply. "Just what do you think you're playing at, boy?"

"But they... " he turned to point at the girls. They were not there. They were all now on the other side of the pool: all save one, who was halfway across, slowly dog-paddling towards the others.

The next thing Howard knew he was being seized by his arm and dragged towards a plastic poolside chair. In the blink of an eye, Miss Parminter was sitting down; and a moment later Howard found himself lying face-down across her knee, staring intently at her white leather tennis-shoes. Then his swimming-trunks were pulled right up tight into his bottom by the waistband and, when he reached back to pull them back down again both of his arms were pinned into the small of his back.

And then—smack! smack! smack! smackety-smackety SMACK! SMACK! SMACK! as a dozen short, sharp, crisp brisk slaps rang out across the pool.

Again, the shrill peep! of the Tivercombe teacher's whistle.

"Girls!" she shouted. "Girls! Just concentrate on what you're meant to be doing. And yes, that means you, Angela; and you too, Deborah; so you can both stop sniggering and wipe those silly smiles off of your faces; and all of you, just look where you're meant to be swimming! Did your parents never teach you that it's very rude to stare?"

Another blast on the whistle.

"Girls! Did you hear me, or am I just speaking to myself?"

It appeared that she was.

"AND YOU, Franklin... " said Miss Parminter as she pushed the pink-bottomed Howard off of her knee—regretting the fact that she had not thought to spread a towel over her gym-skirt before pulling the dripping wet boy over it—"You can jolly well get into that pool right now and join your classmates over on the far side by the diving-boards."

"Girls! Did you hear me, or am I just speaking to myself?" [P. 56]

18. Waiting at the Stable

EACH OF THE doors opening onto the school stable yard had a hand-painted sign attached to it. "Blackie" said one; another said "Samson"; a third read "Charlie"; a fourth "Dapple" and so on and so forth, all of them the names of the horse or pony that lived within: all apart from the last one, that is, which said PRIVATE—NO BOYS in big red letters.

Inside this door, the girls of the horsey set had converted the spare stable into a sort of office or den for themselves. Instead of straw and hay there was a collection of old classroom chairs, and two threadbare old armchairs, one with the stuffing coming out. Instead of water buckets there was a table, which bore the ring-marks of mugs of tea-bag tea and instant coffee, together with a collection of mismatched mugs, an electric kettle and tea-spoons, milk-bottles and suchlike. Hanging from nails in the beams were various rosettes, hats, wax jackets, pony head-collars and items of tack; and in the far corner of the room there were two blue plastic barrels: one, with a makeshift wooden lid on, was used for feed pellets; the other, open-topped, acted as a sort of umbrella-stand for a collection of whips and crops and sticks of various ages and in various states of repair, and besides these, a well-used crook-handled school cane, bound at the end with tape where it had started to fray.

Between rides, girls in jodhpurs lounged on the chairs within, chattering excitedly about jumping and gymkhanas and fetlocks and curry-combs, while outside a small army of junior boys fetched and carried buckets of water and feed, shovelled and mucked out and wheeled barrows to dungheaps, tacked up and untacked, polished and brushed, and generally made themselves useful.

This morning, a bright, fresh Sunday morning, the stables were unusually quiet. Most of the ponies and their riders were out in the fields and bridle-paths. Only Sarah and Laura remained in the den, and both girls seemed restless and agitated, pacing the room, as if they too wanted to be up on their ponies and out. They were dressed for riding: Sarah had on a pale blue roll-neck lambswool sweater with her jodhpurs, rather than her weekday school shirt and tie, and Laura a pair of decidedly un-Regulation fringed buckskin chaps from home, over her English riding kit.

Sarah looked at her watch.

"What time do you have?" said Laura.

"Eight minutes to eleven" said Sarah, swishing her crop.

"Oh." she said. "What time was the last time I asked?"

"Nine minutes to eleven."

The girls were silent. Laura picked the cane from the plastic bucket. It was a thin and whippy one, and much lighter than she imagined a cane would be, and certainly a lot more so than her steel-sprung crop. She flexed it between her fingers—it looped almost double. She examined the end. It seemed such a slight, insubstantial thing, and not at all anything to make such a fuss about. She held out her left palm and flicked the cane smartly across it; and then she yelped and almost jumped out of her boots with the sharp, stinging pain.

"Ow!" she said, rubbing her palm against the side of her leg. "That hurts!"

"Let me see" said Sarah.

There was a faint pink line across Laura's palm.

"Well, what did you want to go and do that for?"

"I don't know... I just wanted to see what it was like, I suppose."

Sarah chuckled.

"Well, now you know." she said.

Laura smiled.

"Yeah, now I know."

She went and looked out of the stable door. Half a dozen junior boys holding brooms were standing talking in the otherwise-empty courtyard. She watched them for a while.

"It's a really nice day out there," she said.

"I know." said Sarah.

"What time did she say she was coming?"

"Eleven."

"And what time is it now?"

"Six minutes to."

Laura stepped out into the courtyard and looked around.

"There's no sign of her yet." she called.

The boys caught sight of the cane that Laura was still holding, and suddenly seemed to remember what their brooms were for. In the space of a few minutes of frantic brushing, they had made a passable attempt at sweeping one small corner of the cobbled yard, and heaped up a small mound of straw and dirt in the process; and then, noticing that Laura seemed to have her mind on other things, and that she was only a third-year anyway, and not entitled to use a cane at all, they left off sweeping and went back to their conversation.

And then there came a sound, like the faint singing of several voices, coming from the fields behind the stable block.

"Sarah... " Laura called.

Sarah came out to listen.

The sound came closer. It was singing. Not very good singing, but singing nevertheless. Or rather, there was one very good voice amongst them, a clear, high female voice, and several bellowing, raucous, tuneless male ones.

"Val-de-reee!" came the sound,

"Val-de-raaaaa" louder and louder and more and more tuneless.

"Val-de-reeeeee!" The two girls looked at each other. The boys in the stable-yard left off their brief flurry of sweeping and stood leaning on their brooms to see what the din was.

"Val-de-ra-HA-HA-HA-HA-HA!"

And with this, at eleven o'clock precisely, to the second, a small, noisy procession rounded the corner of the stable block.

In front strode a fresh-faced, clear-voiced young woman in her twenties, in short khaki shorts and hiking-boots and with her flaxen hair in two plaits over her shoulders. Behind her marched Davies, holding a stethoscope and singing at the top of his voice, and Howard—in long trousers—bellowing with a thermometer in his hand; and then Gudgeon, the loudest and most tuneless singer of all by a long way, weighed down by two large black leather medicine-cases, with sundry appliances and instruments poking out of his pockets, trudging straight through the junior boys' pile of sweepings and spreading them all over the yard again with what looked very much like a deliberate kick.

"Val-de-RE-DA-RE-DA-RAAAAA!" they all yelled as they came to a halt right in front of the girls.

19. Heidi Kraus

THE YOUNG woman with the plaits stepped forward.

"Good mornings" she said, holding out her hand. "Heidi Kraus. I am coming from Zürich and am the new Veterinary Surgeon. You are for the wormings?"

"Yes." said Sarah. "Well, not us personally, but our ponies are."

"Good, good. So, you will lead the way?"

"Yes, of course."

"Good." She turned to the three boys. "And you will be bringing the baggages for me also?"

"Absolutely" said Davies.

"You bet!" said Howard.

"Er… yeah," said Gudgeon.

"This is most excellent." said Heidi Kraus. "You know, these boys they are so kind. They are volunteering for this task, and are of great help already to me also."

"Hmmm." said Sarah, fixing Davies with a long, suspicious stare. Davies gave her an innocent smile back.

"Always keen to help a lady," he said.

"Wouldn't want to see her struggle" said Gudgeon.

"Don't mind how long it takes us" said Howard. "We'll just hang out here while she works, and do whatever we can to help her."

"Hmmmm," said Sarah. "And what were you supposed to be doing instead?"

"I can't rightly remember," said Davies. "Can you, Howard?"

"It might have been a ten-mile compulsory cross-country run, William."

"Oh yes! So it was. And you know how much we like those, don't you, Howard."

"Can't get enough of them, William. But we can't leave a lady to struggle all by herself, can we?"

"Hur-hur-hur" said Gudgeon.

"So," beamed Heidi Kraus. "You are really too kind. Now, let us begin the wormings of horse."

THEY ALL trooped into the stable belonging to Blackie, Sarah's pony, and the vet rifled through her medicine-cabinet, pulling out a brown glass jar of what looked like white gobstoppers, and a sort of oversized pea-shooter. Then she pulled Blackie's mouth open, popped the end of the pea-shooter between his teeth and blew. There was a phut and a dull thud as the gobstopper hit its target, and that was that.

"So," said Heidi Kraus. "Now we are waiting a few instants to make some measurements of temperature and heartbeatings, and to be sure that the pill is not coming out of the mouth once more, and then we are doing the same also to the next horse."

"And then can we ride them?" said Sarah, eagerly. "I mean, we don't have to wait for anything else, do we?"

"You may ride."

"Oh, excellent!"

"And also," said the vet, turning to Davies, who had just pulled an enormous handful of white sugar-lumps out of a paper bag, and was about to cram them into his face. "I would not advise the eating of these items."

His hand froze about half an inch from his mouth, and then he made a great show of inspecting them closely:

"Er... I was just checking they're not... er, broken" he said, unconvincingly

"Checking is fine," said Heidi. "But eating is not fine. Not at all. Eating is very silly. These are my sugar-lumps. My special sugar-lumps, for the horses and ponies which are getting too frisky in the stable and are not letting me carry out the required treatment. You will ask, Heidi, why are these sugar-lumps so special, and I am telling you. These sugar-lumps, you see, you eat one and you are going to sleep, just like that"—she snapped her fingers—"... and no-one is waking you up until many hours have passed; and then your head is hurting very bad. So, not for the schoolboys eating, yes?"

Sarah looked over at Laura, who was still holding the cane she had picked up from the plastic bucket, and then at the vet; and she was just about to say something when there was a knock at the stable door, and one of the senior girls entered: she was a tall, auburn-haired sixth-form prefect by the name of Lisa Alcott.

"I say!" she said. "I'm looking for a cane. Do you have one in here?" And then she spotted it in Laura's hand.

"Ah, there it is. I thought we'd lost it. Do you mind awfully if I borrow it for a moment?"

Sarah looked as if she were about to interject, but then appeared to think better of it.

"Oh, no: you go right ahead," said Laura, offering the cane to the prefect "I... I was just holding it. I didn't mean to bring it with me."

"Thanks!" said Lisa, and off she went.

After some business with the stethoscope and thermometer, Heidi Kraus declared that the worming had been successful, and that they should now do the same for Samson, the pony loaned to Laura, The two girls led her out, leaving the boys to gather up the equipment and follow along behind.

Out in the stable-yard, the junior boys who had been so half-heartedly sweeping the cobbles were now standing in a line in front of the mounting-block, apart from one of them, who half-knelt, half lay across the top of it, his shorts down around his knees. Behind him stood Lisa Alcott, cane in hand.

"You are a lazy, lazy boy!" she was saying.

The vet went through the same procedure with the other pony: the jar of gob-stoppers, the blowpipe, the phut and thud, and the measurements of temperature and heartbeat afterwards; while from outside there came the swish and crack of a cane in use, and a young boy's yoww's and oww's growing steadily higher, and more desperate and more tearful.

"There!" said Heidi Kraus. "This wormings is now done. The horses may now be ridden also."

When they led the two ponies out into the yard, the boy who had been over the block was just getting slowly and tearfully to his feet, clutching tightly at the seat of his white school underpants.

The prefect tucked the cane under her arm, unfastened the next boy's elastic snake-belt and pulled his shorts down with a swift tug.

"You English!" said Heidi, shaking her head.

"Looks like we don't have a mounting-block for a while," said Sarah, as the boy lowered himself over it. "I think we need a substitute. How about… " she looked around her. "Ah yes. Davies! Hands. Now!"

She made him stand at the head end of her pony, slightly crouched down, his hands clasped together, and then she stood facing him, so that her chest almost touched his forehead.

"Oh dear," she said, looking down at her boots. "Those boys don't seem to have made a very good job of sweeping the yard, do they? Look what I've trodden in."

And with this she lifted her left foot and put it into Davies's hands. Then she pressed down with all her weight, twisting her boot as she did so, and sprang up into the saddle.

"And Franklin," she said. "Since you're so keen on volunteering today, Laura needs a hand up, too."

20. An Unexpected Delivery.

WHEN LAURA arrived back at her room, dusty and pleasantly tired from her afternoon's ride, there was a boy in waiting outside her door. He was a short-trousered junior boy, and he was holding a parcel. It was a squat, battered-looking sort of a parcel, awkwardly wrapped in scrappy brown paper and tied up with odd lengths of frayed baling-twine.

"Parcel," said the boy. "From America," he added, drawing Laura's attention to the unmissable patchwork-quilt of small-denomination US Mail stamps that covered at least half the parcel.

"For you." he concluded; and indeed the words TO MIZZ LAURA WALL, LINTON ABBY SCOOL scrawled in thick, black, two-inch-high letters across the paper, pretty much ruled out the possibility that it might be for anyone else.

"Why thank you," said Laura, taking the parcel from him. It was surprisingly weighty for its size.

She turned to her room.

"Excuse me… " said the boy. "But can I have the stamps, please? I mean, when you've finished with them—and if you don't want them—for my collection."

"Say," she said, catching his eye. "Don't I know you from somewhere?"

"Might do," said the boy.

And then she remembered.

"Oh!" she said. "You were the boy who tripped over us in the playground."

"That's right," said the boy. "Edwards is the name. And it was your friend who got so furious with me and sent me off to be punished. Still," he said. "It was my own fault really. I should have looked where I was going."

Laura looked at him, unable to shake from her mind the image of a tearful boy with crimson slap-marks on his face and legs, waiting in a long corridor beside a heavy mahogany door. And also the memory of the muffled thwacks and yelps that echoed throughout the school.

"Did she hit you very hard?" said Laura.

He rubbed his bottom ruefully.

"You can still see the marks, you know. If you look close."

He twisted round and pulled the right leg of his shorts up.

"Do you want to have a look?" he said.

Laura put her parcel down crouched down. The tips of two faint red stripes peeped out from beneath his fingers.

Edwards pulled his shorts higher, revealing the edge of his white school pants and, just beneath these, the start of a third stripe, darker than the first two, and tinged with blue bruising.

"Oh my!" said Laura. Instinctively she reached out and touched the stripe with her finger—it felt slightly rough—and then she realised what she was doing, and pulled her hand quickly away.

"I... I'm sorry" she said, blushing. "I... I didn't mean to touch. I wasn't thinking."

"I wouldn't worry about it," said Edwards. "Blimey! That's nothing: I've had half the girls in my class inspecting the damage, and prodding and poking like anything. Girls seem to like doing that, you know. I suppose it must be interesting for you—I mean, not knowing what it feels like to get it yourself and that. Here," he said, unbuckling his snake-belt. "I'll show you the rest if you want."

And just at that moment there came the sound of a door opening and closing, and the clatter of feet on the staircase, and the chatter of girls' voices; and the very next moment, as Edwards yanked his shorts up straight, Sarah Johnson appeared in the corridor, still in her jodhpurs, together with Katie Atwell and Hilary Carter. Katie had been playing lacrosse, and carried her lacrosse stick with her and wore her lacrosse kit—her short navy kilt and her knee-length navy socks. And although it was a weekend, and although she really didn't have to do it at all, Hilary had been where she almost always was, down among the conical flasks and Bunsen-burners in the chemistry laboratory, with her nose in a textbook and her hands on a rack of test-tubes; and she carried her white school lab-coat over her arm.

Edwards jumped to attention.

"Well, well" said Sarah, looking him slowly up and down. "Delivering the post, are we, boy?"

"Yes, Sarah."

"Anything for me?"

"No, Sarah."

"Pity. Off you go then."

"Yes, Sarah. Thank you, Sarah."

And off he ran.

"Golly!" said Katie, pointing with her lacrosse stick. "Laura's got a parcel!"

21. Uncle Zeke's Gift.

AND A VERY odd parcel it was. Not only did it look odd, with all its stamps and its baling-twine; but it smelt even odder. The tattered brown paper and wadded padding had a smell of wood-smoke about it, and engine-oil and ig-grease and soil and all sorts of other things besides; and as Laura tore into it n the writing-desk in her room, another smell, stronger and more pungent than all of these put together, wafted up from the inside.

"Yikes!" said Katie, wrinkling her freckled nose.

"Yuk!" said Sarah, screwing up her eyes.

"Hmmm… " said Hilary, leaning closer. "Very… er, interesting."

"Oh dear," said Laura. "I think I know what it is."

It was a brown earthenware jug with a cork stopper, and with it there was a hand-written note.

Laura pulled the cork out of the jug, and almost at once the whole room was filled with the throat-constricting, eye-watering smell of…

"Petrol!" said Katie. "Phew, what a stink!"

"Or aviation-fuel" said Hilary.

"Oh, my… " said Laura, embarrassed. "I don't quite know how to put this. It's not gasoline, and it's sure not aviation fuel either."

She pushed the cork firmly back and picked up the note that nestled in the torn-off wrapping-paper.

Dere Laura, [it said], *I shure hope you having a rite nice time at that fancy school over there in England. I seen yore Ma and Pa las week an they both mity proud of you. I always said you had all the brains in this family, cos gosh darn, I sure wernt one for none of that ole book learnin stuff myself.*

I hope they feedin you well. Yore Ma says they dont eat no fried squirrel over there, an dont have no grits neether. So I say to her, what they live on then, and she jus laugh an say, roast beef an york-shire puddn. Now what in the world kinda food is that for a body to eat every day? So anyhows I figgerd you mite want sumthin to wash it down with.

Your ole uncle Zeke. PS I made it myself.

"You see," said Laura. "Uncle Zeke's a real nice man, but… well, he lives up in the mountains and they do things differently there. He doesn't see many other folks where he lives, just other mountain-folks, and he thinks that everyone else likes what he likes. He makes this stuff out of corn and sugar-cane in a big old contraption he built out of an automobile engine. We always thank him for it and act real pleased when he gives it to us, and then Pa uses it to strip paint."

"And... ?" said Sarah. "So what is it, exactly."

Laura took a deep breath.

"Moonshine." she said.

AND MEANWHILE, and not very far away, Matron was out and about on her Sunday afternoon round. And at that very moment Matron was making her way down the staircase towards the very floor where Laura and Sarah had their rooms, scrutinising her nurse's fob-watch as she went, and she was not happy at all.

It was because of the time that Matron was not happy, and because of the three boys in the dorm above.

Matron was nothing if not an orderly woman. There was never so much as a hair out of place on her tight-bunned head, or so much as a speck of dust or a smear of grease on the stout lace-up shoes that graced the ends of her stout, wholly matronly legs. As she descended the staircase, Matron's white apron was, as it always was, a dazzling, cardboard-stiff paragon of starch and cleanliness; but this time all was not as it should have been. This time, the time was thoroughly out of joint, and it made Matron really quite cross indeed.

On Sundays, Matron always descended the staircase at four o'clock—never earlier, and never later—and after a brief tour of the first and ground floors, she retired to her room for tea and biscuits at four fifteen.

But this day it was already four fifteen, and there was still the whole of the first floor to do. This day there had been noises in one of the boys' dorms, and Matron had burst in to find three well-known troublemakers huddled furtively at the far end; and when she had asked them what they were up to they had played innocent with her, and had refused to reveal what they were doing even after being lined up by their beds for some pretty robust, rolled-up-sleeve slapping of their faces and thighs; and in the end, the time being what it was, and her routine already having been thrown quite out, she had been obliged to leave none the wiser, and with nothing but a handful of confiscated white sugar-lumps to show for her efforts.

And now, going down the stairs, she suddenly became aware of the strange, pungent smell wafting up from the floor below.

22. A Narrow Escape.

S ARAH CLOSED the bedroom door and stood with her ear pressed to the wood as Matron set off crossly down the corridor. She stayed there for a long time after the sound died away completely, just to be sure; and when she was sure, she stood up and unbuttoned the ill-fitting white lab-coat that she wore over her riding things.

"She's gone!" she said.

Laura looked up from the diagram she had been studying so intently in the impenetrable chemistry textbook on her writing-desk, and noticed, as she did so, that it had been upside-down all along. She turned it back round: it made no more sense than it did before.

"Phew!" said Sarah. "That was close!"

The door of Laura's wardrobe burst open and Katie and Hilary came tumbling out onto the floor, together with various shoes and clothes and rackets and crops.

"Golly!" said Katie, picking herself up. "I didn't think I could bear it in there a moment longer."

"It really was rather compact, I must say" said Hilary.

"Here," said Sarah, giving Hilary a hand up and giving her back her lab-coat and books. "Thanks for those. They certainly seemed to do the trick!"

"But what I don't understand," said Katie, pulling up one of her long navy Lacrosse socks, which had fallen down around her ankle. "What I don't understand is why you couldn't have just said."

"Said what?" said Sarah. "Said that Laura had illegal alcohol in her room? Said that her own family sent it to her?"

"But do you think Matron really believed all that stuff about it being for your chemistry prep?"

"She thought it odd. But I looked her straight in the eye and told her we'd just finished titrating an oxide of potassium permanganate to neutralise its electrons, or something, and would she like to come and take a closer look,"—she held up the foul-smelling jug—"and not to mind if the fumes discoloured her apron or interfered with her watch, and that soon sent her scuttling off."

"But did she believe you?" said Hilary.

"Of course she did," said Sarah.

The others didn't look so sure.

"Well, she did believe us," said Sarah. "Whatever she might have thought. She has to, because we're girls. We'd hardly tell a lie now, would we?"

There was an uncomfortable silence.

"And what about Edwards?" said Katie, at last. "He delivered the parcel. He must have smelt it. What if he tells on us? And what if they find it here, and they find out we've lied to Matron?"

"He won't." said Sarah, grimly; "Not unless he wants to deliver himself the sorest bottom he's ever had in his entire life."

Whether the others were comforted by that, they didn't say; but it was decided, right there and then, to get rid of the earthenware jug, and its contents, and the wrapping-paper and the twine, and everything else to do with it, and dump them immediately into the big metal dustbins behind the kitchens; which, as luck would have it, were due to be wheeled out into the lane that very afternoon, to be emptied by the council bin-men into their dumper-truck the following morning.

And it just so happened, as luck would have it (though whether the luck was good or ill is quite another matter) that on that particular day, three third-year boys had been allotted the task wheeling the bins out; three boys, in fact, who at that very moment sat, with smarting, smacked thighs and blazing red cheeks, in their dimly-lit dormitory two floors above, examining the two white sugar-lumps that one of them had managed to hide from their confiscating Matron.

And neither Sarah nor Laura—nor Edwards either, for that matter—had any idea of what was going to hit them.

23. Sent to the Head ·

WHEN EDWARDS delivered the bundles of the *Linton Abbey Gazette*, the school magazine, to the bedrooms, studies, dorms and common-rooms of the school, he did not think to open a copy and take a look at the letters page. There was no particular reason why he should, in normal circumstances, and every reason why he shouldn't: if he had been caught standing around reading when he ought to have been working, then, in the words of one of the school *aide-memoires*, A Lazy Boy—as the saying went—Is A Punished Boy.

But it was unfortunate, nonetheless, that he didn't take the chance to read it, just this once: for if he had, he would have understood the shocked looks and the whispers and the pointing in the playground that followed him; and he might have been a little less surprised at the stern and abrupt manner of haughty, pony-tailed girl prefect who sought him out to tell him that his presence was required in the Head's office, at once; or the little knots of girls pointed at him and whispered to each other as he passed, and said things like "The nerve of it," and "the cheek of it!"; or boys eyeing him up with what looked like a mixture of incredulity and—and this was the oddest thing—even a kind of respect. He even came upon three strapping great lads in long trousers striding shoulder-to-shoulder towards him at the school door; who to his utter amazement, actually stood aside to allow him to pass, almost as they would have done for a girl.

"Well done, old chap!" muttered one of them, under his breath.

He might almost have been pleased, were he not so worried, and had he not heard what the other two boys said after he passed.

"He's bonkers!" said the second.

"Absolutely," said the third. "But you've got to hand it to him, for sheer guts."

Then there were two tall fifth-form girls standing by the dining-hall door.

"That's him!" said one.

"Oh, he's really, really going to catch it!" said her friend; "He is going to be so sorry!"

"And serve him right, too!"

He gulped and made his way, as steadily as he could, past them, and on past open classroom doors where the pupils craned their necks after him, towards the Head's study, in which a sixth-form tutorial was under way.

24. Edwards' Letter

"**S**PEAK ROUGHLY to your little boy," said the Head. "and beat him when he sneezes." She looked past the cane on her desk to the three earnest, bright-eyed sixth-form girls who sat on the other side. "He only does it to annoy," she continued. "because he knows it teases." She picked up her cane and pointed to Julia. "Continue." she said.

"Ahem," said Julia, clearing her throat. "I ah, I speak severely to my boy..."

The Head nodded.

"... I beat him when he sneezes."

"Go on," said the Head.

"For he can thoroughly enjoy," said Julia. "The... er, the pepper, Headmistress?"

"Correct."

"The pepper" said Julia. "when he pleases."

"So," said the Head. "And what does it mean, that last phrase?"

"Well," said Julia, turning back the pages of her copy of *Alice in Wonderland*. "In the book, it's a sort of mad scene in the Duchess's kitchen, and the whole room is absolutely full of pepper. Here... "—she read aloud—"'There's certainly too much pepper in that soup,' Alice said to herself, as well as she could for sneezing. 'There was certainly too much of it in the air. Even the Duchess sneezed occasionally...' and so it goes on, Headmistress. It's a reference to the pepper in the room. The cook has put rather too much of it in the soup."

"And that's all?" said the Head. "What did you learn of Victorian nonsense poetry in our last session?"

Emma Hope, a rather clever, but shy and bookish girl, raised her hand.

"Yes, Emma?"

"We learned that Edward Lear's *The Yongy Bongy Bo* was a satire on Tennyson's *The Lady of Shallot*, Headmistress."

"That is correct."

"Oh yes!" said Julia. "And we learned that 'The Aged, Aged Man' in Lewis Carroll is full of references to William Wordsworth. Or was it 'You are Old, Father William'? That was Wordsworth? Or was it Keats?"

"Precisely!" said the Head, who—fancying herself as something of an intellectual, had decided to take a sixth-form English tutorial to prove it; but who had forgotten the precise details herself, having only read them in the English mistress's notes half an hour earlier.

"We must learn to look deeper at poetry." She said. "Consider the characters. Consider... ." She rifled through the crib-sheets prepared for her... "Consider a Duchess: what might she represent?"

Julia raised her hand

"Authority, Headmistress? Tradition?"

"And a cook?"

"An ordinary member of the public?"

"And they are both in agreement about what?"

The third girl, the auburn-haired prefect Lisa Alcott, raised her hand.

"Boys, Headmistress," she said. "How to deal with them."

"Good," said the Head. "And how do these representatives of Victorian public opinion both high and low think that small boys should be dealt with?"

All three girls raised their hands.

"Julia?"

"They think we should speak severely to them, Headmistress."

"And beat them at the smallest provocation." said Lisa.

"And why, pray?"

"Is it because it's in their nature to tease and misbehave?" asked Emma.

"Some things never change," said the Head. "But let us re-examine the last line of the poem in that light. What might the word 'pepper' mean, apart from the spice?"

"I suppose it's sort of hot and stinging," said Julia

"And it brings tears to your eyes," said Lisa

"Ye-es," said the Head. "but of course 'pepper' is a noun as well as a verb. Or should that be an adjective as well as a participle?" Sshe consulted her notes. "But what does it mean, to *pepper* something?"

The girls were silent.

"Think!" said the Head, moving on to territory she was much more comfortable with. "What method of beating small boys was most favoured in the Victorian age?"

At that moment there came a knock at the door.

"Yes!" snapped the Head, rather cross at having been interrupted on the threshold of her specialist area.

"Please, Headmistress," came a muffled voice from behind the door. "I've been sent to see you."

The Head let out a sigh of irritation, and then strode over to the door and jerked it sharply open.

Outside stood Edwards, his bare knees quivering.

"You, boy!" boomed the Head, seizing the lad by the ear and dragging him into the room. "And would you care to explain what the meaning of this?"

"Of... of what, Headmistress?"

The Head snatched up a copy of the school magazine and waved it into the cringing boy's face.

"Of this, boy! Of this!"

"I... I don't know what you mean, Headmistress."

"Oh you don't, do you? Don't play the innocent with me, young man."

"But... but I *don't* know"

"DON'T LIE TO ME, BOY!"

"But... "

"Enough!" She thrust the magazine into Edwards's hand "You will take this, and you will read it out loud, so that these girls can all hear what you have done."

"But what bit of it shall I read, Headmistress?"

The Head appeared to be turning purple.

"This, boy" she exploded, jabbing at the page with her forefinger. "This!"

It was a letter. There was a heading above it, in capitals, which said IT'S NOT FAIR!

Edwards started to read.

"It's not fair!" he read. "Why do girls always get everything they want, and never get punished for anything. And do we boys always have to do whatever they tell us to do all the time, and why do we have to stand up when they come into the room, and carry their bags, and do whatever they tell us to do? And why do we get beaten for every little thing, and why are they allowed to watch, even when we get our trousers pulled down? It's not as if... ." Edwards faltered,.

The Head grabbed her cane and whipped it across the top of her desk.

"Read on!" she said.

"It... it's not as if they're any better behaved than us;" read Edwards. "For example, I happen to know for a fact that a certain stuck-up spoilt brat junior prefect and her clever-clogs American exchange student friend have this very week broken some of the most serious Rules of this school. Of course, I am too polite to go into detail here, or even to name their names, but they know full well who they are, and they know what they have done. And if I were their teacher I would give them both the cane. Really hard. Right across their smarmy girly knickers. Until they cried. So there! Signed... ." Edwards looked up in horror.

"It says... it says signed, EDWARDS. But... but that's... but I never... but it... But I *didn't do it!*" he wailed. "I really, really didn't. You've got to believe me, please you've got to. I beg you... I promise you, I *didn't.*"

"Indeed?" said the Head. "And so I suppose that someone else just happened to write a letter with your name on it, just for the fun of it, did they?"

"They must have... "

The Head slammed her cane across the desk-top again.

"IMPOSSIBLE! As if any pupil at my School—even a boy, however vile and corrupt he may be—would... stoop so low as to invent such... such scurrilous allegations and then blame them on you, a fellow pupil, a fellow boy... why, it is out of the question! Who would do such a thing? What monster? Can you name me even one?"

Now, if Edwards had thought about it, seriously, for about one second, and if he hadn't been paralysed by fear of the furious cane-wielding Headmistress standing before him, and the thought of what she was about to do to him in front of the three pretty sixth-formers who sat looking disapprovingly at him; and if he could have allowed himself to believe the depths of wickedness and depravity to which certain boys would sink, he probably could have come up with not one suggestion, but several. But as it was, he didn't.

"But it must be a mistake" was all he could wail.

"A mistake? A MISTAKE? For your information, young man, I have spoken to the young ladies in question, the young ladies whom you slander so grievously in your letter; and it goes without saying that I have an absolute assurance of their complete blamelessness. Their only 'crime', it seems, was to have reported you to me for your wilful clumsiness in the playground. And so you thought you'd get your revenge on them, did you? By heavens, boy! I wish I had caned you twice as hard that day. I wish I had beaten you to within an inch of your miserable life. But you may rest assured, Edwards, that you will not get off so lightly this time, my lad!"

"Ahem" A polite cough behind her.

The Head turned, suddenly remembering her sixth-formers.

They had their blazers on now, and their copies of Lewis Carroll, and their fountain-pens and fancy girly pencils and coloured plastic rulers and rainbow-hued erasers and pencil-cases were all neatly packed away in their satchels.

"Sorry to interrupt, Headmistress," said Julia. "But if you're busy, we'll er... we'll be off, shall we?"

"You will do nothing of the kind, Julia," said the Head. "I will not have the education of my sixth-formers compromised by the behaviour of this... this... boy! No, I shall deal with him now, and then... "

The Head paused, as if suddenly struck by an idea.

"But wait... " she said. "Perhaps we may make this incident instructive, and relevant to our studies. Do you not agree?"

The sixth-formers were a little puzzled by what she might mean, but they all nodded in agreement nevertheless.

"Splendid!" said the Head. "Now, let me see… "

She hooked her fingers into the boy's waistband and, with a single swift tug, pulled his trousers and his underpants right down around his ankles.

"You will wait here," she said. "And you will not move and inch. Do you understand me, boy?"

"Yes, Headmistress. But… but… "

A ringing slap across his bottom silenced him.

"Now, ladies," she said. "If you will excuse me, I shall be a few minutes.Continue to study while I am gone." and she turned and left the room.

IT WAS A good fifteen minutes before she returned; and when she did, she was wearing a pair of gardening gloves, of all things, and carrying a pair of secateurs in one hand and, in the other, a large bundle of bushy twigs.

"There," she said, spreading the twigs across the top of her desk. "These chaps should do the trick."

And then she set to work. It took her no more than a few minutes to trim the twigs to a uniform length—about two feet—to strip them of their leaves and to bind them all together tightly at their thick ends using a roll of sticky tape, so that they formed a sort of bundle, like a slim witches' broom, without the handle.

This done she swished the bundle through the air a few times, removed some of the side twiglets, and repeated the process a few more times until she was happy with it.

"That's it!" she said. "And who can tell me what it is?"

No answers.

"The ignorance of the young people of today! It's a Birch. Which, as you will no doubt be aware, was the preferred instrument of discipline of the Victorian age."

Three heads bent over three exercise books. Three pens wrote *The Birch*, in neat, round, girlish handwriting, and *Preferred Instrument of Discipline, Victorian Age*.

The bundle of twigs was handed to Edwards, who was instructed to pass it to each of the girls in turn so that they could examine it more closely. Emma Hope nearly died of embarrassment when the half-dressed boy stood before her and offered her the rod: she coughed, and said "thank you" in a hoarse voice, without meeting his eye, and gave the twigs a perfunctory but surprisingly stinging flick across her open palm, before handing it straight back to be passed to Lisa, who flexed it and swished it, and examined the twigs, and weighed it up, and looked keenly from the birch to Edwards's as-yet unmarked flanks and back again, and swished it some more, and showed some considerable interest in the way the boy flinched as she did so.

A spare chair was fetched from a nearby classroom, where a needlework lesson was in progress. A boy was sent to fetch it—Edwards, as it happened—after two sharp strokes of the Head's cane to the bare bottom disabused him of the impression he had that he might be allowed to dress himself first.

The chair was placed in the centre of the Head's study and Edwards was bent across the back of it, his bare bottom facing the sixth-formers, but far enough away from them to allow the Head to take a decent swing without any of them accidentally catching a glancing blow. Then, without further ceremony, the Head raised the birch high above her head and whipped it hard—*swittt!*—right across the boy's upturned bottom.

He squealed and wriggled, and tried to grab his rump, which almost immediately had acquired several broad stripes of bright, mottled red.

A second stroke followed a few seconds later, and then a third, and a fourth, and then a fifth and a sixth—switt! switt! switt!—each slightly harder and quicker than the last as the Head got into her stride; and the boy's squeals grew from pained to piercing to tearful to desperate and pleading, to great heavy sobs, to whimpering; and still the strokes came—switt! switt! switt!—without let-up.

At length, the Head paused to examine her work.

"Hmm!" she said, crouching down and prodding the crimson flesh. "Hmmm... not quite there. Perhaps if I... " and she fiddled with the bundle of twigs, pulling them back into shape here and pruning away extraneous side-twigs there, and swishing the rod through the air.

"Ah!" she said. "That's the trick!"

And then she performed a little rising-and-falling limbering-up exercise with her right shoulder, rolled her head once to the right and once to the left, and drew the birch right back, and brought it down with such a force that Edwards and his chair were physically shifted a good two inches forwards, and little fragments of twig flew out across the room. The boy let out along wail of anguish, which rose several octaves as the next stroke lashed his bottom, and the next and the next and the next and the next.

"There!" said the Head at last, putting down what remained of the frayed birch-rod, and pointing to Edwards's bottom. "Now take a look: come on, come on! He won't bite you."

He squealed and wriggled, and tried to grab his rump. [P. 76]

The girls closed their books, brushed the fine sprinkling of bark and twig fragments from their hair and their dresses, and stood up to see what it was that the Head wanted them to look at.

JULIA FOUND THE references later that evening in her study, as she sat at her writing-desk in her cotton pyjamas with a pile of books and a mug of steaming cocoa.

The first came from the dictionary. "To pepper," it said. "To sprinkle liberally or to pelt, e.g. with shot". She copied the words out into her exercise book, and saw again, in her mind's eye, the sharp, frayed ends of the bundle of birch-twigs, and the dozens upon dozens of angry little purple marks that peppered—yes, peppered, she thought—the sobbing boy's whipped bottom.

The second was the entry in Brewer's *Phrase and Fable*. There was just one entry for the word: it read "To pepper one well. To give one a good basting or thrashing."

25. Another Tea-Party

SARAH LEANED BACK in her fireside chair.

"I just feel so… " she stopped.

Davies, in his usual corner, stood perfectly still, with his nose pressed to the wall and Sarah's book balanced on his head. He didn't fidget, or huff and sigh, or cough, or do any of the other countless little irritating things he usually did to annoy the two girls.

"He's listening," she said.

Laura looked up, and then turned to look around at the half-open bathroom door, where Howard was at work. He was right by the door, in exactly the same position he had been in the last time she looked, slowly polishing exactly the same patch of floor.

"They both are."

Sarah let out a cry of frustration.

"Davies! Out!" she said, picking up a plimsoll. "Out! I'm sick of the sight of you."

She flung the plimsoll across the room at him. It missed.

"Charming, I'm sure," he said, as one of Sarah's framed photographs crashed to the ground. "Are you sure you wouldn't like me to stay and clear up this broken glass? No? Absolutely sure? Oh well, so I suppose I'm free to go back to my dorm now?"

"No you are not! You can… Oh, you can go and make us a pot of tea, you hateful boy! And take him with you."

"It will be my pleasure." he said.

Sarah slammed the door after them and threw herself back down in her arm-chair.

"I just feel," she said. "I just feel as if people are looking at us, talking about us behind our backs, trying to work out what we've done wrong."

"We should have just told Matron about the moonshine," said Laura. "She would have understood. It would have been all over by now."

"It should have been. We threw the stuff away. Oh, that horrible, horrible brat

Edwards! How did he know? Why did he have to write that awful letter? What was he thinking of? I swear, I am going to make life so hard for him he'll wish he'd never been born! He is going to be reported for every little thing he does, every single day. He is going to be spanked so much!"

"I don't think... " said Laura. "I don't think it was him."

"What?" said Sarah, incredulous.

"Well, he seems like such a nice kid. Sure, he's a boy: sure he gets into trouble—boys do. He makes a noise, he bumps into people, he takes too long to do things sometimes. He gets the cane, like they all do. But he wouldn't do something like that... he's just not the kind."

"And what about all those things he said about girls, and about us?"

"I just can't believe he would have done that."

"Laura, he put his name on the letter."

"*Someone* put his name on the letter."

"But he admitted doing it. He stood up in front our class and apologised for it. You heard him yourself."

"Yes, but he'd been dragged there by his ear. He had his pants down. He was in tears. The Principal was standing behind him with a cane in one hand and a bunch of switches in the other. Sure he admitted it. But I would, too: wouldn't you?"

"Laura, you're far too gullible where boys are concerned. You think, if a boy's nice and polite to you one day, that he really wants to be nice and polite, and that he's always going to be like that: but they're not like that at all. They really aren't. They're not like girls at all. If you'd lived with brothers like I have you'd realise. Oh, you really would. Most of the time they used to treat me like they hated me, and they'd never let me play their games, however much I pleaded with them. I even cried, and they just laughed at me; and then sometimes, all of a sudden, it would be like they'd had a complete change of personality, and they'd say 'How are you, Sarah?' and 'Come and play with us, Sarah' and 'Would you like a lick of my lolly, Sarah?', and I would be so happy; and then they'd snatch the lolly away when I went to lick it, and run off laughing; or I'd catch them whispering behind my back and it would turn out that they'd spat on it first. The only times they were ever nice to me was when they wanted something from me, or when they were trying to trick me, or when mummy spanked them to make them be nice to me. And the minute the stinging faded, they were back to their old selves again. Laura, believe me: all boys are hateful. They need to be spanked. And that is exactly what needs to happen to Edwards."

"But what if he really didn't do it? What if someone else—another boy—did it to get him in trouble. What if that boy did it to get us in trouble?"

"But who would hate us that much? And who else could have known about… well, about us having the you-know-what?"

There was a knock—rat-a-tat-tat—at the door.

"Room service!" said a smarmy voice.

And in came Davies, carrying a large wooden tray, on which were arranged two china cups and saucers, two teaspoons, a fat, white china teapot and a jug of milk. And behind him came Howard, with a tablecloth over his arm; and in his hand he held a small, round bowl containing just two, slightly battered-looking, white sugar-lumps.

26. Morning

AS THE GREY, misty dawn broke, the great slumbering school lay still and quiet, its heavy double-doors and tall curtained windows closed to the outside world. Outside in the fields the ponies stood patiently in the dewy grass, whilst on the verges and by the hedges, early rabbits peeped and scuttled. A wood-pigeon called, its coo-coo COO coo-coo echoing across the empty hockey pitches.

Down the lane, in the gatehouse cottage, a solitary oil-lamp spluttered into life, and a short time later there came the sizzle and splutter of frying bacon, and then the scrape and clatter of a knife and fork on a china plate.

A door opened and Jenkins the groundsman emerged into the morning mist, wearing a battered oilskin coat.

Over at the school a bell rang twice. Footsteps echoed along a corridor and climbed a staircase, and then, one by one, the curtains and windows of the upper-floor boys' dormitories were flung open wide, and there came the rush and rumble of boys' footsteps, hurrying to stand by their beds before.... .

THUMP! The sound of a boy falling—or being pushed—from his bed. And SLAP! And a yelp. And SLAP! again, but this time sharper, as on bare skin, as if an intervening layer of cloth—pyjama bottoms, say—had been pulled out of the way.

Down below, on the lower floors, the first few bedside lamps were switched on, and, a little later, the first few heavy-curtained tall sash windows, were opened; and the girls opening them could be seen: some in school pyjamas; some in various stages of dress and undress in uniforms or sports kits or jodhpurs.

As he reached the school courtyard, Jenkins unbuttoned his oilskin. The sun was visible now above the treetops. He noticed that the two bedroom windows directly above the main doors remained closed and curtained. Normally they were open by now: normally their occupants were amongst the early risers, up and out long before breakfast. Often they passed him, pink-faced and jodhpur'd, on their way to the stables. Such polite girls, too: always acknowledged him—"Morning, Jenkins" they'd say; and he'd stand aside to allow them to pass, and doff his cap and tap his forelock and say "Morning, Miss Sarah" and "Morning, Miss Laura", and "Lovely day today, young Misses" if it were a nice day, or "Miserable day today, young Misses" if it weren't. But today their curtains were closed. "Probably need their beauty sleep," he thought. "Bless 'em".

Broken glass. There was broken glass on the ground.

The rumble of feet and the scraping and banging of stacking chairs being unstacked and arranged in rows and blocks all down one side—the right-hand side—of the assembly hall. As usual, the left-hand side remained open and empty and chair-free. A lectern was pulled to the centre of the stage, and a row of chairs arranged behind it. The Head's heavy carved wooden armchair was pulled by four hefty boys to the middle of the row.

Down at the stables now the first of the pony set had begun to gather in their PRIVATE—NO BOYS den. Tack was examined. Mugs of tea were made and consumed. Feed-buckets were filled. The auburn-haired prefect Lisa Alcott sat on a hay-bale, thoughtfully examining the frayed end of the crook-handled cane from the plastic bucket.

And out in the fields, two uncollected ponies chewed at the grass.

THE SUN climbed higher in the sky.

BREAKFAST. Followed by...

ASSEMBLY. The filing-in of pupils, girls first, boys after, in order of age and seniority. The clamour of voices rising and swelling and then ending in an abrupt and perfect silence as the teachers took to the stage.

Then came the Head, gowned and capped and bearing her cane, and looking even sterner and more serious than usual. She surveyed the school from her lectern: it was divided like the red sea, with a clear path between the two sides; the boys to the left, standing—the smaller boys in their shorts at the front, the taller boys in their long trousers at the back—and the girls seated, in their summer dresses and their blazers and their ankle-socks, and their ribbons and plaits and pony-tails and bunches, in their rows and blocks of seats to the right.

"We shall sing Hymn number 23" she said, gruffly. "*The Lord is My Shepherd.*"

Two empty seats, next to each other, halfway back, amongst the third-year girls.

"*For Tho-ou art with me a-and thy rod and sta-aff me comfort still!*" sang the school.

"It has been reported to me," said the Head, when the singing was over. "that there were noises heard in the school after lights-out last night. The sound of laughter was distinctly heard, and a great deal of banging and crashing. I have the distinct impression that school property was being damaged. Unfortunately, Matron was unable to apprehend the culprits in time."

She paused, and glared over at the standing boys.

"But they need not imagine for one moment that they have got away with it!" she smacked her cane across the top of the lectern, and half the school gulped and flinched involuntarily.

"I shall expect the pupil or pupils responsible to report to my office immediately after assembly. Is that understood? Oh yes, we shall get to the bottom of this, if I have to thrash every single boy in this school!" Which she had done before, and on more than one occasion.

JENKINS, MEANWHILE, returned with a galvanised tin bucket and a stiff wooden broom. The broken glass was flat, as if it came from a window. He looked up: yes, there it was—up in young Miss Sarah's sash: one of the panes was smashed right out.

27. A Wake-up Call

L AURA WALL DREAMT of home. She dreamt of the clapboard farmhouse with its timber shingles and its rickety porch, and the chickens scratching in the yard, and the big old wood-framed barn where the hogs lived in winter, and the dirt road that led across the grasslands towards where the grey hazy mountains met the blue open sky. Outside, her pony chewed the grass contentedly while English schoolboys in grey shorts and rolled-up shirtsleeves saddled him up with her old Western saddle. Only they weren't English boys at all: she recognised them all, the worst boys from her local school, every one of them—there was buck-toothed, nose-picking Billy-Bob from the Ewing farm, and Jimmy-Ray and Duwayne, the pinching, pigtail-pulling Chandler boys, and Jeremiah and Obadiah Taylor, the tell-tale sons of the local Baptist preacher, and the nasty little barefoot Jaycee Budd from the trailer park, half your height but cocksure as you please— kick your shins as soon as look at you, with five mean-as-hell big brothers to back him up, and an even-meaner-than-that Pa in and out of jail all the time.

Meanwhile, an auburn-haired girl-prefect stood behind them with a crook-handled cane with a frayed tip, saying "You lazy, lazy boys!", and whipping them harder than hard across their bottoms and legs whenever any of them came within arm's reach.

And then she was riding through the tall, dry Summer grass, and into the wood beyond, sending the black-and-white ground-squirrels scampering for cover before her. The path grew narrower and narrower, and the wood darker and darker and the ground rose upward and upward. Mountain country. The pony slowed to a walk, and then a steady uphill plod. She had a feeling as if someone was following her, over to one side in the undergrowth, just beyond her vision. A tree rustled. She turned and glimpsed a dark shape vanishing into the trees—was it a brown bear? Or someone... someone who for some strange reason reminded her of Howard, or his friend Davies, or both together. She kicked her pony on, and gave him a smack on the rump with—what?—not a green switch from a wayside bush or tree but a white, rubber-soled plimsoll from her Linton Abbey P.E. kit.

Up ahead there was a wisp of blue smoke rising through the trees, and a faint tinny sound, as if from a transistor radio. Yes, it was! She could hear the strains of a slide guitar and banjo. And somehow the sound was a comfort to her, and she could sense the presence in the woods—whatever it was—holding back, afraid to approach.

"You are listening," said a voice. "To WLAR., the Home of Country." and then she rounded a big rock to see the cabin, Uncle Zeke's cabin; and Uncle Zeke was there, chopping logs in his patched denim dungarees and his high lace-up boots and his orange hunting cap.

"Well, I'll be!" he cried, standing up and spreading his arms wide. "If it ain't little Laura!"

The boys from the farm were there now, too, all lined up to the left of the woodshed door, looking pale and nervous. There was a hickory stick hanging over the lintel, and two junior girls in cotton socks and summer dresses were climbing onto a stacking school chair to fetch it down for someone—she could not see who—who was inside.

"You don't pay them no mind," said Uncle Zeke. "You hear me?"

And then they were past the woodshed, and in Uncle Zeke's cabin, in the dim light and the wood-smoke, the black cooking pot bubbling away on the range, the gun-rack on the wall.

"I done made this for y'all," Uncle Zeke was saying. He was holding a brown earthenware jar. "Y'all go ahead now."

He unfastened the stopper, and all at once the cabin was filled with the pungent, eye-watering smell of moonshine. He poured a little into a white Linton Abbey teacup and offered it to her.

"Here, drink yourself some."

"Oh, but Uncle Zeke," Laura said. "It's awful nice of you, but I can't. It's against the School Rules."

"Heck! Rules don't mean shoot here. This is mountain country."

He pressed the cup on her. She tried to refuse, and took a step backwards, and as she did so she tripped and her hand caught the cup as she fell. Then she was flat on her back on the floor, and the feel and the smell and the taste of the moonshine was everywhere: all over her clothes, in her hair; even in her mouth.

And all the shuttered windows flew open, and there were boys looking in, hundreds of boys, all laughing at her. Jimmy-Ray Chandler was there, and Jaycee Budd, and all the other local boys, and Howard Franklin too, and Davies, and Gudgeon, and the three of them were laughing loudest of all.

And then there was a tremendous banging at the cabin door, and then a rattle and a jangle, and the sound of a key turning in the lock, and then Matron was there, shaking her, saying "What is the meaning of this?" over and over again.

AND THEN SHE woke up, flat on her back in Sarah's room, and the room was strewn with broken plates and furniture, and the bedclothes were ripped, and there was ink on the walls, and the smell and the taste of the moonshine was still all around her, and Matron was still there, shaking her; and a crowd of boys were staring in through the open door, and she could see Howard, and Davies, and Gudgeon amongst them, and Sarah was sitting on her bed, her head in her hands. And by her side was an empty brown earthenware jug.

"And what," said Matron, picking up the jug and wincing at the smell. "is the meaning of THIS?"

28. Dies Iræ

"You, young lady," boomed the Head. "will wait *here*."

"Yes, ma'am," said Laura, timidly.

"And you, Madam,"—she grabbed Sarah rather roughly by her upper arm—"Will wait *there*. And you will not speak, neither of you; and you will not fidget, and I will see you when I am ready to do so."

And she turned on her heel and disappeared into her study, slamming the door behind her.

THIS HAD NEVER happened before; not ever in the entire history of the school: girls—and not one girl, but two—being made to wait in the punishment queue outside the Head's office. And not only were they in the queue: they were put right at the very end of it, right at the very back, behind almost a dozen boys. The only concession made to their sex at all was that they were given classroom chairs to sit on, while the boys were made to stand; but that was small consolation indeed; and when the sound of footsteps approached, and the doors at the end of the corridor burst open, and groups of girls and boys passed by on their way to and from other parts of the school; and when they stopped dead in their tracks at the sight of the two girls waiting there, and gave them such strange looks, and when they nudged each other and whispered to each other, Laura almost, almost wished that she had been made to stand facing the wall like a boy, because at least then she wouldn't have been able to see them.

The Head's door was thick, and the walls were even thicker, but in the silence of the corridor the pupils in the queue could make out what was happening in the study. There would be a gabble of muffled voices, one deep and severe and commanding, the other higher and pleading and protesting and promising; and then four booming syllables, audible even through the timber and stone: "Bend over, Boy!" And then, after a dreadful pause, the whoosh-thwack! sound of caning, or the swish-splat! sound of strapping, or both, and the rising yelps of a boy in pain. Then the door would open, and a red-faced, tear-streaked boy would limp out, take a quick glance at the others in the queue, and dart off back down the corridor, back to his class or back to his gym or lab or sports-pitch; and the Head would call "Next" from her study, and the next boy would take a deep breath and step reluctantly in; and the door would close and the queue would move along, and Sarah and Laura would have to pick up their chairs—all by themselves—and move them along a few paces and sit back down again.

And so it went on, for an hour or more; until, at last, there were no more boys left; and the great door opened and the Head came out, still holding her cane. She glared at the two girls for what seemed an eternity.

"I will see you now." she said.

29. Expelled!

"YOU MAY COUNT yourselves lucky" said the Head.

The two girls did not feel very lucky at all: in fact, standing there on the rug before the great mahogany desk, they probably felt less lucky, and more miserable, at that moment than at any time in their entire lives.

And this after twenty minutes of towering, red-faced fury, in which the Head had risen from her chair and told them, eyeball-to-eyeball, that they should count themselves disgraces to the name of their school, a shame upon their sex, and disgusting little liars, amongst other things.

"Do you know why you should count yourselves lucky? Do you? Do you, eh?"

They couldn't even begin to imagine why.

Sarah stared at the carpet, clenching the hem of her blazer between whitened knuckles, biting her lip. Laura started to cry.

"That's enough of that from you, young lady! Tears will get you nowhere with me. You will stop it this instant, do you hear me? And you—look at me when I'm talking to you! Now, I shall tell you why, since you obviously aren't going to tell me. You may count yourselves lucky that you are not boys. Because if you were"— she picked up a cane from her desk—"Why, if you were I should strip the pair of you of the uniforms that you are so unfit to wear—every last shred of them—and by Heaven I should thrash you both so hard in front of the entire school that you would not walk—much less sit down—for a month of Sundays. That is what I would do to you. I simply cannot begin to comprehend the depth of your wickedness... Drunkenness!"—THWACK! the cane slammed down on the desktop— "Vandalism!"—THWACK!—"Dishonesty!"—THWACK!—"Deviousness!"— THWACK!—"And to cap it all, you both continue to deny it even now, to my face, with the smell of alcohol on your breath. The nerve of it! The cheek of it!" THWACK! THWACK!

Knock-knock!

The Head spun around on her heel.

Knock-knock! again, at the door.

"Excuse me, Headmistress" came a muffled voice from outside.

The head strode over and flung the door wide open.

It was Edwards.

"I've just come to deliver the... " he began; but the Head wasn't listening. In a flash, she had seized him fiercely by the ear, dragged him across the room to her desk, flung him over it and yanked his shorts and pants down.

"Interrupt me, will you, boy? I'll teach you!" she cried, raising her cane high above her head.

"But Headmistress…

THWACK!

"Owwww! But… ."

THWACK!

"Aaah! But I only… "

THWACK!

THWACK!

THWACK!

"Yowwwww! The post… "

THWACK!

"Pleeease!"

THWACK!

"I'll teach you some manners!"

THWACK!

"I'll teach you some respect!"

THWACK!

"I'll teach you what's what in this school!"

THWACK!

THWACK!

THWACK!

And then she grabbed the sobbing boy by the ear again and propelled him across the room and out into the corridor, throwing his shorts and pants after him.

"And stay out!" she said, and slammed the door.

"And as for you," she said, turning and advancing on the girls again. "You are expelled. Finished. You will be escorted to your rooms, where you will remain until arrangements are made to remove you from the premises. Oh, and Miss Johnson… "

The Head walked up to Sarah and seized the enamel Prefect badge on her dress.

"I will take that."

And with a ping of a breaking pin and a little rip of tearing of cloth it was gone.

30. Waiting To Leave.

L AURA WALL, ALONE in her bare room, on the edge of the bed, her head in her hands, her whole body shuddering with silent sobs, her entire worldly posses-sions packed in a single, battered suitcase.

SARAH JOHNSON, STARING pale-faced out of the tall sash window in her summer dress—torn at the chest where her Prefect badge had been so harshly ripped away—clenching and unclenching her fists; her riding-boots and jodhpurs, her hacking-jacket and crop, all packed away in the blue nylon sports-bag that sat on top of the metal trunk containing her books and pens and clothes, her gym-skirt and plimsolls, her comb and her wooden-backed hairbrush.

HOWARD J. FRANKLIN III, William Marmaduke Davies and Gudgeon (just Gudgeon), out in the playtime courtyard beneath Laura and Sarah's windows, aware of Sarah's gaze and of the sounds carrying upwards to the girls' rooms, dancing wildly round and round in circles singing na na-na na-na NA!, na na-na na-na NA! and miming drunken staggering and falling over, and laughing and laughing at the tops of their voices.

FLAXEN-HAIRED KATIE Atwell, in her tennis kit, and carrot-topped lab-coated Hilary Carter, striding away from the distasteful spectacle, towards the shade of the great Cedar of Lebanon where the courtyard ended and the lawns began; and only stopping on the way to briefly speak to an auburn-haired girl prefect—Lisa Alcott—and to point her towards where the three boys were, before continuing on their way.

"I don't believe it!" said Katie, spreading her tennis sweatshirt on the grass and sitting down. "I really don't."

"I don't want to believe it" said Hilary. "But what other possible explanation can there be? They were caught red-handed, flat out on the floor and stinking of alcohol. And not any old alcohol, but the moonshine that Laura's uncle sent her."

"But they threw it away. In the bins."

"They said they threw it away. Obviously they didn't."

"But what if someone got it out of the bins and tricked them into drinking it?"

"What, made them drink it? And then erased all of their memories of it?"

"Well, what if someone slipped it into their tea or something. When they weren't looking?"

"Katie, you can smell it in the next room, with the door shut and the lid on. The chances of anyone just 'slipping' it anywhere without anyone noticing it are, quite frankly, rather remote. You'd probably find it easier to 'slip' the entire science lab into someone's tea, if you ask me."

Katie poked at her tennis-shoe with the end of her racquet.

"Well, what if… what if someone got the jug out of the bin, and kept it hidden away somewhere, and then what if they slipped something else into their tea, so that it knocked them out, and then what if they went and got the moonshine from wherever they had it hidden, and poured it all over them and into their mouths, to make it look like they'd drunk it, and what if… " Katie stopped. This was all getting far too far-fetched, even for someone so desperate to believe.

"You mean, what if space-aliens did it?" said Hilary. "Or fairies? Or flying pigs? Of course, it's possible… Lots of things are possible, but… Have you ever heard of Occam's Razor?"

"I've heard of Gillette, and Wilkinson's Sword, if those are any good."

"No, Occam's Razor is something we have in science. It's the principle that if you're faced with a choice of explanations for something you don't really understand, you always go for the simplest one. Which, in this case, is… "

Katie swiped hard at a dandelion clock. "Guilty as charged."

LISA ALCOTT WAS puzzled. She had slapped the three boys good and hard, smart and sharp, right across their silly faces, forehand and backhand, side-to-side, CRACK! CRACK! CRACK! CRACK!, one-two-three-four; but all it had done was to make them worse. They'd yelled, of course, but they'd yelled like they were doing it on purpose, like they were playing up to it, like they were enjoying the opportunity to cause a disturbance beneath the windows of the two disgraced girls.

"YOWW!" they'd shouted, and "YOWEE!", and "YAROO!" and "YIKES! THAT WAS A STINGER!", And "OH NO—IT'S MY TURN NEXT! I REALLY HOPE IT DOESN'T HURT!" as if they were doing it for a pantomime, as if it were all a big game.

So she'd slapped them all the harder, leaving all sorts of handprints, but it had only seemed to encourage them all the more. Slapped silly and flaming red, the boys had grinned and yelled like chimps, and drew an ever-bigger crowd with their antics; and in the end she'd had to send them off back to their lessons.

Rubbing her poor, aching, crimson palms against her cotton dress, she watched them lolloping off towards the main entrance, unaccountably still sniggering.

Up in the room above, Sarah Johnson turned away from the window and flung herself down on her bed.

31. The Plot Thickens

"I THINK IT'S barbaric," said Edwards. "The way they've treated those two girls. Just barbaric."

He stopped for a moment in the corridor to rearrange Katie's sports bag and satchel over his shoulders, and her blazer and straw hat under his arm, and his own things in his right hand and Katie's lacrosse stick in his left. Katie waited for him, tall and long-legged in her lacrosse kit.

"I mean," he said. "Girls aren't meant to be treated like that. You just aren't designed to be treated roughly, are you?"

Katie, a good head taller than Edwards and a great deal more athletic, shook her head.

"I feel so sorry for them both," he said. "Poor things."

They reached the door that led out into the playground and to the lacrosse pitch beyond. Katie, walking a few paces in front of the boy, reached it first. She waited for him to catch up and then to unload himself of all his baggages once more, to hold the door open for her.

"Thank you, Edwards," she said, as she walked through. The door swung shut behind her. Edwards, loaded up again, managed to open the door for himself by barging at it, and catching the handle with his elbow.

"I mean," he said, struggling to catch up with the blonde-haired athlete. "I dare say I've been treated pretty roughly in my time… "

Katie stopped and allowed the boy to pass her, and as he did so her eyes flicked idly down at the backs of his legs; where, peeping out beneath his shorts, she could make out the results of various slappings and canings.

"I know," she said.

"But most of the time I've deserved it; and even when I haven't, there's been other things I've done and got away with, so it all works out alright in the end; but to shout at girls like the Head did: I mean, really shout at them, and them being so delicate and feminine and all; and to make them actually wait in the punishment queue, behind boys—well, I just can't believe it. No-one can. And do you know what?"

"What?"

"I don't think they did it. Oh, I know they were supposed to have been caught red-handed and everything, but look at me—they said I was caught red-handed about that letter to the school paper. It even had my name on it, and the writing even looked like mine, but I didn't do it. No-one will ever believe me, of course, but I know what I know, and I know I didn't write a word of it."

Katie stopped in her tracks.

"Honestly?" she asked. "I mean, really and truly, cross-your-heart-and-hope-to-die honestly?"

"Honestly. Really and truly, cross my heart and hope to die."

"Golly!"

"And the thing is, that letter that I was supposed to have written was about those same two girls, from someone who knew they were going to get in trouble. Someone doesn't like them. And someone wants to hurt them, at any cost."

"But what about the way they were found, smelling of alcohol and everything?"

Edwards put down his baggages and moved closer to Katie.

"I think they were *framed*," he said, in a low, conspiratorial voice. "I think someone slipped something into their tea, and then turned over their room, and then poured that stuff all over them."

"But who would do such a thing?"

"Val-de-ree!" the sound of raucous singing close at hand.

"I don't know," said Edwards, picking up Katie's things again. "But all I know is, someone did it."

Katie set off across the playground, leaving Edwards to follow her.

"Val-de-raa!" Three boys turned the corner in a row, swerved slightly to miss Katie and barged straight into Edwards, sending him flat on his back and scattering his bags all around him.

"Oops!" said Davies. "Didn't see you there."

Edwards didn't hear. He was writhing on the ground, clutching his thigh.

"Oh dear" said Gudgeon. "I seem to have kneed you in the leg. By mistake. As you do."

"Oh well," said Howard. "These things happen. Too bad. You'd better pick up your bags. Don't want to be late for your lesson now, do you? You might get another caning."

And all three of them burst into a fit of sniggers and giggles, as if Howard had just said the funniest thing in the world.

"No!" said Katie, standing behind them with her hands on her hips. "You'd better pick them up—those were *my* things. In fact, Edwards can go now and you three can bring them. And if you're late for your lesson: well, that's just too bad, isn't it? You'll just have to take the consequences, won't you?"

32. Occam's Razor

"**A**ND SO YOU see, Headmistress," said Katie. "Laura and Sarah would already have been unconscious by the time whoever it was that did it came back with the jug of alcohol; and so when he—or they—smashed up the room, and made it look as if they had been drinking, they wouldn't have known a thing about it."

"And," said Edwards. "it's no wonder that they can't remember anything that happened. It's not that they're lying, and it's not that the drink has wiped their memories out: they would never have been aware of any of it in the first place."

"I've been doing some research," said Hilary. "And I've concluded that there are any number of chemicals—medical and veterinary tranquillisers—that could have been slipped into the girls' food or drink without them ever being aware of it; and in a matter of seconds they would have been totally insensible."

The Head looked long and hard at the three eager faces before her in the great panelled study.

On the wall, above the framed diplomas and fifty years or more of formal school photographs, a railway-station clock ticked away the seconds and minutes.

From outside there came the faint ringing of the playtime bell.

"This," said the Head at last. "is the most preposterous explanation I have ever heard in all my years of teaching. It is pure nonsense. Sheer and utter nonsense."

"But Headmistress… " said Katie.

"Do you seriously expect me to believe such a thing? Do you really believe it yourself?"

"Of course, Headmistress?"

"And even you, Hilary?"

"I didn't, but I do now."

"Have you not heard of Wilkinson's Sword?"

"Do you mean Occam's Razor, Headmistress?"

"I Mean What I Mean," said the Head, grandly. "Nothing more and nothing less. And I will thank you not to question me."

"Yes, Headmistress. Sorry, Headmistress."

"If I did not know you better, and if I did not know that you were both serious girls, I would say that you were having a joke at my expense. And as for you... "

She picked up her cane and pointed it to Edwards.

"Did you put these girls up to this? Did you? Is this your little game, eh, boy? Make these girls look fools in front of me? Make me look a fool in front of the lot of you?"

Edwards shrank back, terrified.

"Oh no, Headmistress!" said Katie, stepping in front of him. "It was my idea first and foremost. Really it was. He just confirmed what I already thought."

"Hmmph! A likely story! And I suppose he told you that someone else wrote that letter to the school magazine, did he? And that he had nothing at all to do with it? Well? Well? Eh?"

Katie was silent.

"It is break-time," said the Head. "I suggest that you two girls go out into the playground and do whatever it is that you do there. And I want you to forget all of this nonsense once and for all. Do you understand me?"

The girls nodded.

"You may go."

They turned to leave.

"And you, Edwards,"—the boy's eyes darted in growing panic from the departing girls to the Head, and the cane she flexed menacingly between her fingers—"You will stay."

EDWARDS LAY face-down on a towel on Katie's bed, his trousers and underpants in a little heap on the floor, wincing as the long-legged athlete dabbed at the mass of raised welts with a sponge dipped in ice water from a small china bowl.

"It's broken the skin there," she said.

Hilary leaned over to look.

"So it has," she said, prodding the boy's bottom. "And there, too; and there across the tops of his thighs."

Edwards winced and bit his lip as the two girls examined the damage.

"Golly!" said Katie. "I bet it really hurt! I'm so glad I'm not a boy!"

"High-strength tranquillisers!" said Hilary, suddenly. "Where would we get them from?"

"Are you sure?" said Katie. "I mean, that's a bit over-the-top, isn't it? I'd thought of a dab of witch-hazel on it, or liniment or something... "

"No, not for him—I mean, in general, if someone wanted to get hold of tranquillisers to drug someone with, where would they go?"

"Someone medical, I suppose. Maybe the doctor's surgery in Tivercombe."

"Or what about the local vet," said Edwards. "We could maybe phone them to see if they've dispensed any at the school lately, or if any have gone missing."

"But it's very not likely, is it?" said Hilary. "I mean, you would have thought they'd have noticed if someone stole their drugs. And besides, who at this school would have gone all the way to Tivercombe and burgled a vet's surgery? No, I think we're looking for something much closer to home."

"Hmmm… " said Katie. "What about Matron's medicine-chest?"

"Of course!" said Hilary. "So what we need is someone to go and ask Matron if she's given any tranquillisers to anyone, or if any have gone missing. Now, who could that person be?"

And two pairs of eyes turned to the boy on the bed.

33. A Cup of Tea

"AND OF course," said the Head. "I raise this just as a possibility, you understand. But as the hour of their final exclusion from this school approaches, it occurs to me that it would be best to consider every possibility, no matter how incredible it may seem; and you, Miss Clark, as their form teacher, and you, Julia, as their Head Girl, may tell me if you think it at all likely that they may have been... ahem, drugged, by person or persons unknown, and 'fitted down', as the expression has it... "

"Er... 'fitted up', Headmistress?" ventured Julia.

"Young woman, the precise direction of the fitting is neither here nor there; and I will thank you to confine your observations to the relevant issues. What I am seeking is your opinion on the general principle of the thing."

Miss Clark cleared her throat to speak; and it is likely that the philosophical principle of Occam's Razor would have got yet another airing, had there not been a knock at the door at that precise moment.

"Tea, Headmistress!"

It was Matron.

Julia opened the door, and in she came, with a tray of tea and biscuits.

"Perhaps," said the Head. "We should ask Matron for her opinion on this matter."

"You ask ahead," she said, as she laid the cups out on the Head's desk. "Always willing to help."

"Now, Matron, it concerns Miss Johnson and Miss Wall... "

"Oh, it's a shocking thing, isn't it?" said Matron. "What those two girls did. And they seemed such nice girls, too. Always polite, always cheerful, as if butter wouldn't melt in their mouths. Milk, Miss Clark? But I was wise to them, of course. Oh yes, I knew their little game. Do you know, they lied to me about that... that alcohol they had in their rooms. I sniffed it out, you see. Biscuit, Julia? But I knew they had something there. I smelt it. And do you know what they told me? They said it was chemicals, for an experiment! And they expected me to believe that! They must have thought I was born yesterday. They must have thought I'd just stepped off of the banana boat. They must have thought I was completely stupid. They must have... ."

"But you *did* believe it?" said Julia. "I mean, at the time you must have, not to report them, or confiscate it."

"Well, yes. But that's not the point." And at this point, Matron thought it wise to change the subject.

"Do you know," she said. "I've heard rumours being put about. Rumours that those two little madams are innocent. There are people seriously saying that someone drugged the little minxes and fitted them up... Honestly! As if anyone with an ounce of sense would believe anything of the kind! Do you know, a young boy even had the nerve to approach me today, to ask me whether anyone might have stolen some tranquillisers from my medicine-cabinet. Well! I dealt with him, I can tell you! He won't be sitting down in a hurry, and that's for sure. But these... these two disgraceful girls, they hide illicit alcohol, and tell lies about it, and then they get caught drunk and stinking of it, with their rooms in a terrible state, and people are saying, it wasn't them, you know: someone else did it. Well, I won't say what I think of that, but I think it's the stupidest thing anyone could possibly believe. To even entertain the idea for a moment! Still, Headmistress, there's one born every minute I say. Now, what was it you wanted to ask me?"

"Ah... No matter. It was not important."

"Oh, I don't mind if it's important or not. You just go ahead and ask me, Headmistress."

"No, really. It was nothing."

"No you ask ahead. Nothing's too little for me to help you out with."

There was an awkward silence.

"I think," said Miss Clark. "that we could all do with a nice cup of tea. That will put us all in fine shape. *Mens sana*, as they say, *in corpore sano*. Eh, Headmistress?"

"What's that? Mens thingy. Yes, yes... *Cogito Ergo Sum*, eh, Miss Clark? *Per Ardua Ad Astra* and all that. And *Honi Soit Qui Mal Y Pense*. I'm a bit of a dab hand with the old Latin tags myself, you know. *Répondez s'il vous plait* eh, what? And a cup of tea would be splendid."

And so Matron got out the tea-strainer and poured the Head a nice, steaming cup of Darjeeling with a dash of milk, just as she liked it, and passed her the sugar-bowl; and the Head picked up the silver tongs and took out three slightly battered-looking white sugar-lumps and dropped them—one, two, three—into her cup, and gave them a stir with the Apostle tea-spoon; and then she took a long sip of the brew.

"Ahhh" she said. "Now that is truly delicious!"

And she took another sip, and another, and another, while Matron busied herself with pouring out the tea for the others.

"There," she said at last. "Now, Headmistress, what was it you wanted to ask me? Headmistress? Headmistress?"

But the Head didn't answer.

Nor did she respond to the sudden knocking at her door—rat-a-tat rat-a-tat-tat; or the prefect's voice calling her from the corridor outside.

"Excuse me Headmistress,"—the voice of Lisa Alcott—"I'm terribly, terribly sorry to interrupt, but it's very urgent. There's a vet at the main door, and she's with Katie Atwell and Hilary Carter and Edwards, and she says that three of your boys have stolen some things of hers, and that they're very important, and she's not going away till she gets them back; and she says that if you don't come out and see her this instant she's going to march right in and... Oh no! she's coming up the corridor now!"

But the Head deep in the bottom-most depths of the deepest deep sleep, said nothing at all; and heard nothing and saw nothing, except in the dreams she dreamed, which were of administration and education and hockey and caning; and nor did she move, at all, except, when Matron shook her, to slump forward insensible onto her great mahogany desk.

"And where," said pigtail-haired Heidi Kraus, standing in the Head's doorway with her hands on her khaki-shorted hips. "are my sugar-lump *medizin-tabletten?*"

34. Last Day

L AURA WALL STOOD at the tall sash window of her big, white room, looking out into the broad, sunlit courtyard of the school that she thought she would never see again.

Turning back to where her friends sat, she caught sight of her reflection in her fireplace mirror one more time, and one more time she saw her new self there: not a West Virginia farm-girl in patched dungarees any more, but an English school-girl, a genuine English schoolgirl, looking right back at her.

Laura Wall was a real English schoolgirl now, and a very pretty one, too: tall and slender and clear-skinned in her starched-and-ironed navy-and-white gingham summer dress and her whiter-than-white ankle-socks, her black T-bar shoes polished to a mirror shine. Her yellow hair shone sleek and glossy in its two long bunches, tied in pretty bows with new two blue ribbons, and it smelt of shampoo and brushing. She grinned and wrinkled her upturned nose: the English girl in the mirror grinned back and wrinkled her nose, too.

"I say!" said her friend Sarah, sitting on the edge of the bed. "You do look splendid!"

And so she did; and so did Sarah, too, in her brand-new school dress, fresh from the cellophane packet, delivered by motor-car at the School's expense from the School Outfitters in Tivercombe; and where the little rip had so recently been, in her old dress, now there shone a brand-new green-and-gold enamel Prefect badge.

The two girls smiled; and so did Katie and Hilary, sitting in the fireside arm-chairs sipping tea and eating digestive biscuits and slices of cake from china plates; and so did Edwards too, standing by the mantelpiece in his flannel shorts, holding the tea-tray.

And down below, the last, painful scenes of three boys' time at Linton Abbey played themselves out, as blinded by tears and stripped to their white Regulation vests, they were led by their ears through the pointing, whispering corridors and stairways of the School, bent and beaten on the bare in classroom after thwack-echoing packed silent classroom; until at last the main doors were flung wide open

They were led by their ears…[P. 102]

and they were flung by prefects, one by one, out into the courtyard. Blubbering Gudgeon—out!—thump! onto the cobblestones, you thug, you dolt, you dimwit; blubbery Davies—be off with you, fat boy!—down the stone steps; Franklin— fraud, liar, brat—and never, ever come back, do you hear? Pelted with their clothes and shoes, the boys cowered on the ground. And, last of all, to cheers from the open windows and doors of Linton Abbey school, a great leather suitcase—one, two, three, heave!—came sailing down the steps, bursting open as it hit the ground and scattering Hershey bars and Marvel comics all around. And Jenkins drove up in the school car, and bundled them in, and such of their clothes and possessions as he could be bothered to pick up and bundle in after them; and then they were gone, for ever and ever and ever.

35. Epilogue

"So," said Sarah, from where she sat on the edge of Laura's bed. "just the one last time, then?"

"Just the one last time," agreed Edwards.

"Who's it going to be?"

"I think it ought to be Laura," said Hilary.

"Absolutely!" said Katie, shaking out her flaxen hair and brushing cake-crumbs off of her short, white pleated tennis-skirt and her long, lean, sun-browned legs. "She is a guest in this school, and after everything she's been through, I think it's only right that she should be the one. It's the least we can do."

"Edwards?" said Sarah.

"Laura," he said. "Definitely Laura."

"But... " protested Laura. "But I... I never... I don't know how to... Aw, gee," she smiled. "Yeah, why not?"

Laura put down her teacup and her plate and made her way to the writing-desk chair that Sarah had placed in the centre of the room. She sat down and smoothed out her dress.

Edwards, now standing before her, unfastened the buckle of his elastic snake-belt.

"For old times' sake," said Laura.

"For old times' sake."

And, as Sarah and Katie and Hilary watched, Edwards eased his shorts down over his hips and let them fall around his ankles. He stood, patiently, as Laura reached out—hesitantly at first—and did the same to his white cotton Y-fronts.

"There you go!" she said.

"There you go," he repeated.

Laura looked up at Edwards and nodded. There was a little lump in her throat as the boy lowered himself across her lap. Gently she turned back the white shirt-tail and tucked it under the bottom of his jumper.

"Ready then?" She raised her open palm over the smooth, bare bottom.

"Ready!" he said.

There was a pause as she looked around at the faces of her friends, friends she thought, so recently, she would never see ever again.

And—smack! and smack! and smack! smack! smack! smack! smack!

Edwards let out a little "Ow!" under his breath, and lifted his right foot a few inches.

"Hurt yet?"

"A bit, Laura," said Edwards.

"Good kid"

And smack! smack! smack! smack! smack! SMACK! and SMACK!
She raised her hand higher and brought it down harder.
Smackety-SMACK! smackety-SMACK! SMACK! SMACK! as the boy's in
bottom jiggled and bounced.

"Ow!" he said. "That did hurt!"

"Me, too," said Laura, looking at her reddened palm. "I guess I'm not used to
it."

"Sorry about that."

"That's okay."

"I think... " said Sarah, crossing the room and picking up her heavy ebony-
backed hairbrush. "I think this might help."

Laura eyed it up doubtfully.

"Oh my!" she said. "Are you sure?"

"Try it."

"It's a right stinger," came the muffled voice of Edwards from below.

Laura weighed the brush up in her hand, drew it back and—WHAP!—smacked
the flat wooden oval hard and sharp across Edwards' bottom.

"YOW!" he exclaimed. "That really, *really* hurt!" As if by magic the shape of the
brush appeared on his bare skin, first white and then a deep and deepening
crimson.

"Yeah," said Laura, examining the wooden surface. "It's kinda got a swing to it."
She raised it again.

Whap! Whap! WHAP!

"OWWWWW!" the boy's feet drummed against the floor, and his hands flew
back behind him to clutch at his bottom, only to be intercepted by Sarah, who
grabbed them and pushed them tightly into the small of his back. He tried to raise
his feet up to protect himself, but Katie seized them and held them down on the
floor.

"Ready?" said Laura.

Edwards' breathing was hard and fast.

"If you say so," he said, through gritted teeth.

Whap! Whap! WHAP!—"A-howww!"

Laura looked up at her friends.

"I'm getting into the rhythm of it now" she said, smiling.

Whap! Whap! WHAP!—"A-haaaaow!"

Laura paused and looked at the wooden brush in her hand.

"Funny," she said. "But it feels kinda natural after a while."

Whap! Whap! Whap! WHAP! WHAP!

"Oh, please!" the boy entreated. "Pleease that's enough now. I can't take any more—I really, really can't. It hurts so much."

Laura became aware of Sarah looking up at her.

"They always say that," she said.

Laura smiled.

"I know."

WHAPPP!— "Aowwwww!"—Whap! Whap! Whap! WHAPP ! WHAPPPP!

WHEN THE spanking was over, Laura let Edwards stand up, and gave him a little hug while the other girls inspected the damage, and ruffled his hair—now wet with sweat—and took out her own white cotton handkerchief from her blazer pocket and dabbed away his tears. His top button had come undone, and his tie was all askew. She sorted them out for him.

"There!" she said. "That should put you right."

"Th-thank you, Laura," he sniffed.

"Last time ever!" she said.

"Last time ever," said Edwards.

"Golly, Laura!" said Katie. "You should see what you've done!"

Sarah crouched down to take a closer look.

"I didn't know you had it in you!" she said, impressed.

"Neither did I!" said Laura; and they all laughed, and even Edwards joined in, although it was hard to tell quite whether he was laughing or crying, or both together.

Laura hugged him again.

"Thanks for everything," she said.

WHEN EDWARDS HAD dressed himself he took out from his pocket the envelope the Head had given him, and unfolded the crested notepaper inside, and spread it out on the writing-desk.

The girls crowded round to take a closer look.

"To Whom It May Concern," it said. "In respect of Undeserved Punishments, and in respect of Assistance provided to certain Young Ladies, this Credit Note is issued to EDWARDS, to be presented to Staff and Prefects of this School in lieu of Punishment, in payment for Misdemeanours to the Value of… " and went on to list the value: an enormous number of slaps and cuffs, and slipperings and sundry tannings, and strokes of the cane and birch; and altogether more or less as many, in fact, as an averagely well-behaved boy like Edwards would normally expect to receive during the whole course of his career at a school like Linton Abbey.

Edwards, in effect, had such a mountain of credit that he was unlikely ever to be spanked at school again.

"Golly!" said Katie.

"Gosh!" said Sarah.

"Remarkable!" said Hilary.

"Aw, wow!" said Laura. "And it couldn't have happened to a nicer kid."

She seized him affectionately by both ears and planted a smacker of a kiss on his forehead.

"Well, thanks," said Edwards, visibly swelling with pride.

"You make sure you behave yourself!" said Katie, giving him a playful smack across the bottom.

"And don't get too big for your boots," said Sarah, who, for all her gratitude to the boy, was still a little dubious about the whole thing.

"Oh, I know my place." said Edwards. "I mean, I know my place, Miss Sarah."

"Good. Make sure you do."

"It's funny... " said Edwards. "... You know, I'll sort of miss it, in a way, getting whacked. Not from the Head, of course, or Miss Clark or most of the teachers and prefects, or anything like that; but from you lot, letting me know where I stand. Because it feels a bit scary, having a complete free run at things, and not being punished whatever you do, and only yourself to account to. I don't know how you girls cope, with no-one to say, Stop! That's enough! and smacking your bottoms, and setting you back on the right track again. You're brought up to it, I suppose. D'you know, I almost, almost wouldn't mind it, credit note or no credit note, if I had someone like Laura"—he rubbed his bottom—"To sort me out if I went too far. Keep me on the rails and that."

"Really?" said Laura. "You mean that?"

"Really."

"In that case... " said Laura, looking over to the corner of the room where her steel-sprung riding-crop lay. "In that case, *boy*, I don't think you stirred my tea properly just now. Do you, boy?"

"No," said the boy. "I don't think I did."

THE END